BETTIE PRIVATE INVESTIGATOR SHORT STORY COLLECTION VOLUME 4

CONNOR WHITELEY

No part of this book may be reproduced in any form or by any electronic or mechanical means. Including information storage, and retrieval systems, without written permission from the author except for the use of brief quotations in a book review.

This book is NOT legal, professional, medical, financial or any type of official advice.

Any questions about the book, rights licensing, or to contact the author, please email connorwhiteley@connorwhiteley.net

Copyright © 2024 CONNOR WHITELEY

All rights reserved.

DEDICATION
Thank you to all my readers without you I couldn't do what I love.

INVITATIONS TO SECRETS, LIES AND DECEIT
2nd December 2022
Canterbury, England

No one thinks about the walls.

Before Private Eye Bettie English had fallen in love, before she had become President of The British Private Eye Federation and before she had given birth to two amazing kids, Bettie actually got a lot of cases through strange invitations. Hell, she loved it and she had gotten some of her best and most exciting cases from invitations from mystery senders.

But as she sat at a massive oak round table with only four other people she was really starting to regret her joy of receiving weird invitations.

The dining room she sat in was rather nice and almost magical in a way with beautiful red, green and bright pink tinsel hanging all over the walls and ceiling and the tinsel shined like stars off the crystal chandelier (that was probably real), Bettie had seen some impressive families do great on their Christmas decorations but this family might have topped it.

There of course wasn't one or two or even three massive pine trees in the dining room, there was one in each corner. And Bettie was amazed that each Christmas tree was decorated in an identical way with rainbow coloured LED lights gently pulsing Christmas magic, golden tinsel hugging the tree loosely and little naked candles burning on the trees filling the air with the sweet scents of frankincense and myrrh.

Bettie wasn't exactly sure why the hell these four people wanted to burn naked candles on their trees (surely they knew that was a fiery death sentence) but Bettie didn't really want to argue.

Not when she had received a very panicked letter two hours ago wanting her to attend because someone was going to die tonight.

Bettie had originally planned to spend the night with her amazing, sexy boyfriend Graham as they went through all the great (and utterly rubbish) Christmas decorations that her 70-year-old mum had given her and then Bettie was going to read her two little angels a Christmas bedtime story before she put them to bed (but them sleeping when she wanted them to was a joke at this moment. Four-month-old babies didn't like sleeping).

But the invitation had changed those plans in a flash.

"Welcome everyone," the very tall woman,

probably 32, at the head of the table said with a massive smile.

Bettie rather liked the woman's blue jeans, white shirt and shoeless feet, because it made her look normal and calm and like she was there to make sure everyone had a good time. It was just a shame that the other people at the table didn't look like that.

The other three people at the table were tall middle-aged men and wow did they look the part, and not the good or normal part, the three men were dressed in what Bettie could only describe as "grandad clothes" with their tan slacks, monocle and knitted red jumpers that looked so old they were about to fall apart.

Bettie was looking forward to seeing what these people were meeting about, and most importantly who was going to die. Something Bettie was hoping beyond hope that she could stop.

"We all know why we are here tonight," the tall woman said. "Three years ago, my father Lord Admiral Collins of the British Royal navy disappeared,"

"Happy Collins Day," the three men returned.

Bettie was shocked that she was actually attending Collins Day. She had read about it in the paper recently because his daughter, Beatrice and presumably the tall woman was her, had been launching new campaigns in search of information about her father's disappearance.

Bettie had even had a crack at the case whilst she was on maternity leave during those extremely precious moments when her beautiful angels were finally sleeping.

The case was as strange as it got. Mr Collins had been on leave from the Navy for a month because Beatrice was getting married to the love of her life and Collins wanted to be there for the wedding and Christmas and New Year.

So he left the Naval Base at Portsmouth, England and drove to Canterbury two hours away, he kissed his wife hello and quickly popped to the shops to get some wine to celebrate his return (that was his wife's idea) and then he was never seen again.

There were no witnesses, no security footage that saw him on the second of December 2019 and his wife never heard from him again.

"Beatrice," Bettie said leaning forward, "why did your mother not get the wine?"

Everyone just looked at Bettie like she was a crazy woman.

"Who are you?" the oldest of the three men asked and Bettie noticed a minor scar under his chin like he had been punched there.

"This is Bettie English, the best private eye in the UK and somehow *she* received an invitation tonight," Beatrice said.

Bettie forced herself not to seem surprised at that comment. She was sure that if anyone had requested her presence tonight it would be Beatrice, but she certainly didn't invite Bettie with *that* tone.

"My question," Bettie said again, not really caring for the group's concern towards her.

"My mother was a woman in her late fifties who had just broken her leg after she fell down the stairs. She could barely let my father into the house let alone getting some wine," Beatrice said.

Bettie slowly nodded. That made sense.

"Nibbles Mrs Collins," a man said behind Bettie.

Bettie turned around and smiled when a very young man, maybe 19, walked in wearing a black waiter's uniform carrying a large silver tray of wine, freshly roasted nuts and smoked salmon.

Bettie loved all of those things but one part of herself she had never gotten back after her pregnancy was the ability to eat animal products. Bettie forced herself not to react to the amazing smell of the salmon despite her stomach churning.

Clearly these people didn't know about the possible death threat as the waiter placed the wine and nuts and salmon on the table and then bought out five silver plates and cutlery for them to enjoy the salmon on.

Bettie was starting to wonder if the person who actually invited her was really at the table.

"Are you not drinking Miss English?" the waiter said with concern edging his voice.

"No thank you," Bettie said. "I'm driving and I have two kids at home so I don't anymore,"

"Oh please Bettie," Beatrice said. "This wine is from the hills of Southern France, an area that my father loved. This is how we honour him on Collins Day,"

Bettie politely nodded and pretended to take a sip or two but she did not. The waiter just smiled at her and Bettie was almost a little concerned that everyone wanted her to drink. What if there was poison or something in the wine?

"What have you discovered about my father?" Beatrice asked the three men.

The youngest of the middle-aged man who Bettie was only realising now had a black eye smiled at Beatrice.

"We found one person who remembers selling your father a bottle of wine on the night in question," he said.

Bettie leant forward. "How? I didn't think the Police or Military police found anyone,"

The man with the scar under his chin sighed. "It's a great shame of our society that time loosen up tongues a lot better than a murder,"

Don't say that," Beatrice said. "My father is not dead,"

"My apologies Mrs Collins,"

That was a strange comment and now Bettie was seriously starting to wonder how the hell these people all knew each other. Bettie had believed they were friends or something but surely friends use first names and not formal surnames?

Beatrice started coughing a little and holding her stomach.

"Are you okay?" Bettie asked standing up.

Beatrice took a sip of the wine and smiled as she started picking at her salmon a little.

Bettie really wasn't liking this situation at all. She felt like a fish out of water but the mother angle was still annoying Bettie.

"Beatrice," Bettie said, "is this the same house that your mother lived in all those years ago?"

Beatrice coughed a little more and nodded before picking up a massive chunk of flaky salmon and eating it.

Bettie paced around the wooden table a little. "I assume your mother would have been in here with similar decorations when your father rang the doorbell,"

"Of course," Beatrice said grinning. "These are even the exact same decorations that were up on the night of the disappearance,"

Bettie almost felt sorry for Beatrice because she was clearly so obsessed with finding what happened to her father that Bettie was concerned she didn't have much of a life outside this hunt for the truth.

If Beatrice's mother had told the truth to the police then there was another problem, if she really had broken her leg and was on crutches then Bettie had to admit the mother was strong to walk herself all the way to the front door.

"I hadn't focused on it before," Bettie said, "but your dining room is at the back of the house and you cannot walk straight through the hallway to get from the front door to the dining room,"

Beatrice slammed her fork down on the table.

"You have to go through a number of other rooms with lots of twists and turns and this house probably has tons of hollow walls. If your mother really did that then why wasn't she more tired? And where was the waiter?"

The three men looked at Beatrice and nodded.

"You seem to be obsessed with keeping everything the same so there had to be a waiter, probably the same waiter, three years ago. Why didn't he answer the door? Or better yet, why didn't your father open the door with his front door keys?"

Beatrice downed her wine in a single gulp. "I don't know damn you. I don't know what happened to my father. I don't know what happened to my mother that night. I don't know anything,"

Bettie went over to her and folded her arms. "What do you mean you don't know what happened to your mother that night? Did she lie to the police?"

All three men stood up and went over to Beatrice. Their arms folded.

Beatrice held her stomach a little tighter. "My mother was out that night. She texted my father saying she would be home soon so he went to get the wine as a surprise,"

Bettie looked at the men. "She was having an

affair, wasn't she?"

"No. No. No," Beatrice said. "That ain't true. My mummy was not having an affair,"

The last of the men that Bettie hadn't focused at all on yet just looked to the ground. And Bettie noticed his massive balding patch.

"How long did you sleep with her mother?" Bettie asked calmly.

Beatrice folded her arms and looked like she was about to cry.

"I didn't mean to sleep with her," he said not daring to look up. "I didn't mean to have sex with her. I didn't mean, well, any of it,"

Beatrice hissed a little.

"It was just my wife left me years ago, your mother was so nice and she was annoyed at the Navy for always taking her husband away from her. We were both lonely," he said.

"Damn you Jasper," Beatrice said.

Bettie went over to Jasper and gently raised his head with a single finger. "Did you kill Mr Collins?"

Jasper didn't even smile like that was a stupid thing to say, instead he simply shook his head as his eyes turned wet and Bettie knew, really knew that he was telling the truth.

Someone collapsed to the ground.

Bettie spun around.

The man with the black eye was gasping for air.

Bettie laid him perfectly straight, tried for a pulse

and she didn't find one.

"Call an ambulance!" Bettie shouted.

Bettie immediately started CPR as hard and fast as she could.

Moments later the man gasped as air rushed into his lungs but he didn't open his eyes or move. But he was breathing and for now that would have to do.

Bettie picked him up and placed him gently back into his chair allowing him to lay unconscious, with his head tilted to one side so in case he vomited he wouldn't choke on it.

"I called an ambulance. They'll be here in the next hour," Beatrice said.

Bettie laughed because that really was a testament to how bad the ambulance service was getting in the UK.

"What's going on?" Jasper asked.

Bettie looked at the half-eaten plates of salmon plus her own intact plate and Bettie shook her head.

The food had to be poisoned but it also made no sense. Why poison that particular man? Why not poison Jasper or Beatrice or even herself?

Hell maybe they had poisoned Bettie.

"The waiter," Bettie said. "He smiled at me before he left and at the time I thought he was smiling at me because he knew I wasn't drinking. What if he was smiling because I was about to die?"

Beatrice shrugged. "Look at Tom's wine,"

Bettie presumed Tom was the black-eye man and Beatrice was right, Tom hadn't touched his wine so the poison hadn't come from there.

Bettie waved her hands in the air. "So I received an invitation two hours ago saying someone was going to die and they needed my help to stop it,"

"Great job you did," Beatrice said.

"Did any of you send the invitation?" Bettie asked.

The three people just looked at each other like none of them would dare do such a thing.

Bettie had to agree with them. If any of them had sent the invitation they would have known not to drink or eat or touch anything just in case poison was being used.

"So we have three problems to solve," Bettie said. "I need to know who sent me the invitation, what happened to your father and who tried to kill Tom here,"

Both Jasper, the man with the scar under the chin and Beatrice laughed.

"I'm sorry," Bettie said to the man with the scar. "What's your name?"

The man laughed. "Believe it or not, I'm the uncle of the family. Jeremiah Collins, the bum of the family who has apparently never accomplished anything in my life,"

Beatrice hissed and Bettie thought she was actually going to spit at him, there was definitely no love lost between them.

"How did you get your scar?" Bettie asked.

Bettie loved watching all the colour drain from Jeremiah's face.

"Um," he said. "I was cleaning snow off my drive two years ago and the shovel hit me,"

"We didn't have snow two years ago," Bettie said.

"And you had that scar… three years ago but not before," Beatrice said.

"Fine," Jeremiah said trying to go for the hallway but the waiter appeared and blocked him. "I saw my brother that night he disappeared,"

"And you never said anything," Beatrice said trying to control her rage. Bettie took a few steps back just in case she lashed out.

"I was scared. I met my brother at the house that night and paid the waiter a thousand pounds the next day to say I wasn't,"

"And you still work here?" Bettie asked to the waiter.

The waiter smiled. "I love the family and I actually love the work,"

Bettie was surprised but the waiter seemed nice enough.

"I met my brother here after he found out about the affair because his wife had sent nudes to him instead of Jasper,"

Jasper looked as if he was about to die and really wanted the ground to swallow him up. Bettie loved hearing about people's secrets.

"I never wanted anything to happen but it simply

turned into a massive argument. I said just divorce the woman but he didn't believe in divorce,"

"So you kept pressing daddy and he swung at you," Beatrice said as she rubbed her left arm.

"When did the argument happen? Before or after he went out to get the wine?" Bettie asked.

"After and we never drunk the wine. He was saving it for the wife,"

Bettie was glad these people were revealing their secrets to her because at least the night of the 2nd December 2019 was starting to make sense.

Mr Collins travelled home after deployment to find his home empty and his wife said she was on her way back so he goes out to get a bottle of wine, then Collins received a series of nude photos of his wife that wasn't meant for him and he suddenly realises she was having an affair.

Yet Bettie couldn't understand another question now, what had happened to the wine?

"I need to speak to your mother," Bettie said to Beatrice with a lot more force than she intended to.

Beatrice looked at the ground. "You can't. She's… fragile. She isn't right in the head. And she… isn't a fan of Collins Day,"

"My boyfriend is a cop. One call from me and he will come running and he will investigate all of this including the assault from Jeremiah, the affair and everything else," Bettie said.

Beatrice stood up perfectly straight so Bettie

knew there was more secrets to uncover but she believed that everyone was allowed to have at least secrets to themselves. Hell she certainly did.

"I took her to a home yesterday," Beatrice said. "She has advanced dementia for the past year and a half. She kept thinking that the waiter was my father and, nothing has been going well for her,"

Well that was another dead end for the case.

Bettie just looked at poor unconscious Tom and really hoped that when the ambulance and paramedics got here she could have them run a little test for her.

She needed to know exactly what poison had tried to kill Tom.

Yet Bettie was still no closer to knowing who had wanted her here tonight, who had tried to kill Tom and most importantly what had happened to Mr Collins.

***

Bettie's boyfriend Graham had to be the sexiest man alive and she seriously loved Senior Scientist Zoey Quill because she had agreed to go late into the lab tonight to run a few tests for Bettie, Bettie was definitely going to have to buy Zoey and her husband and her children a very special present for Christmas.

A few hours later, Bettie was sitting at the wooden table again with Beatrice, Jasper and Jeremiah with the air still smelling of fresh salmon, freshly roasted pecans and strong bitter coffee that the waiter had just bought out when her phone buzzed with the test results.

There was no way in hell that Bettie could even pronounce or read the name of the toxin used against Tom but thankfully (and because Zoey was so amazing) she had included a layman's version of the toxin.

"A very rare nerve agent was placed into the salmon tonight," Bettie said. "And this particular nerve agent has to be programmed with the DNA of the victim before it activates,"

"So we're safe?" Jasper and Jeremiah asked at the same time.

Bettie nodded but was still a little surprised that Jeremiah was Beatrice's uncle yet she had been hissing, coughing and holding her stomach all night like she had been poisoned.

"What's wrong with your stomach?" Bettie asked knowing that she really needed to get answers now.

Beatrice looked past Bettie and weakly at the young waiter. Bettie didn't know whether to be concerned or not that it was fair to say the waiter had gotten Beatrice pregnant.

"That's why you stay as the waiter," Bettie said. That made a lot of sense but the nerve agent could only have come from one source that was possible for Bettie to understand.

The waiter went over, stood next to Beatrice and kissed her. And it was nice to see that they were in true love and not some fling that had ended in a pregnancy.

"Did your father ever bring back things from the Navy?" Bettie asked.

Beatrice held the waiter's hand so tight that her knuckles had turned white. "Yes, he bought back little things but he always kept them locked in a safe,"

Bettie just laughed because she finally realised what was going on, how someone had tried to kill Tom and what had happened to Mr Collins three years ago.

Someone, not Mr Collins, was living in the walls.

"Have you ever heard sounds in the walls?" Bettie asked. "Have you ever heard sounds like someone was walking about at night?"

Beatrice's eyes widened. "My mother... she said someone pushed her down the stairs when she broke her leg I never believed her. I lied about when she broke her leg but she did break it four months before my father disappeared,"

"And my brother constantly moaned about food going missing," Jeremiah said. "Nothing weird has happened for years though. No food or anything,"

Bettie just nodded. "This old house has a lot of hollow spaces in-between the walls and I think if we open up some of these walls then we'll find something very disturbing,"

"You think... my daddy's inside?" Beatrice said.

Bettie took out her phone and called Graham. She didn't have the heart to agree with Beatrice but they did need a team of crime scene techs here immediately.

There was a lot of answers to find. No matter how disturbing they might be.

***

The constant low sounds of crime scene techs in their white uniforms, police sirens and Beatrice and the two remaining men giving statements filled the air as Bettie stood there outside in the icy cold winter night with her beautiful sexy Graham standing next to her.

Thankfully he was wearing a massive thick coat that Bettie clung to in case it would warm her up, Bettie was just glad that their little angels were asleep with Bettie's nephew Sean and his boyfriend harry watching over them. At least they were warm and toasty tonight.

Despite all the police cars and white crime scene vans outside, Bettie was still pleased that Beatrice's house looked beautiful and Christmassy outside as it had earlier with plenty of gravity-defying light displays in the shapes of angels, reindeer and snowmen. It was like you were about to walk into a winter wonderland.

And not a house filled with lies, deceit and secrets.

Graham's phone buzzed, took it out and gasped before showing the photo to Bettie. Bettie was amazed that the crime scene techs had found an entire network of narrow spaces in-between the old walls with remains of food wrappings, matches and water bottles littered throughout.

Yet the photo was of the perfectly mummified body of Mr Collins who was wrapped up tightly in a tarp and stuffed at the end of one of the passages that the person living inside the walls had made for themselves.

Bettie felt so disgusted because it was flat out wrong for someone to live inside the walls instead of living in their own house. The things this person could have seen was a horrific invasion of privacy but at least it explained a lot.

It explained why Beatrice's mother had said a man pushed her down the stairs, it explained why Mr Collins' brother didn't know what had happened to his brother after he left and what had happened to the wine, and it finally explained what happened to Mr Collins the night of the 2nd December 2019.

"What do you think happened that night?" Graham asked as he finished texting the crime scene techs because apparently the scene was far too busy, fragile and chaotic to risk Graham contaminating it.

"I think the man or woman came out the walls looking for food that night. He found Mr Collins angry and frustrated about his wife's affair and Mr Collins caught him or her. There was a fight and Mr Collins died," Bettie said.

"Then the killer took him into the walls to avoid anyone finding the body. But just imagine living with your own murder victim for so long?" Graham asked.

Bettie just laughed. "Babe, you realise what we

do for a living. And you think a man living in the walls is the weirdest?"

"Fair point," Graham said, kissing her on the head.

"But where is the man or woman now?" Bettie asked. "And we know what happened to Mr Collins but what happened to Tom and who invited me?"

"Detective!" a uniformed officer standing by the police tape shouted to Graham and then the officer gestured to a man engulfed in the shadow of the bright streetlamps.

Graham waved him through and Bettie instantly knew who this man was. He was the man living in the walls.

Bettie just stared at the very, almost dangerously thin man walk towards them, he was clean-shaved, in good health and looked rather handsome for a man in his late fifties.

The man was wearing black jogging bottoms, a very nice red t-shirt and a thick puffer jacket that suited him perfectly.

"Why kill him?" Bettie asked. Graham didn't seem to be following.

"I never meant to do that Miss English," the man said. "I was made homeless after my divorce and I had nothing but I was once a bricklayer and my father worked on this house,"

"So you knew about the gaps in the wall," Bettie said.

"Of course and my father was a cowboy builder. He didn't put in any insulation or anything so it was hardly a health hazard,"

"It's still illegal," Graham said.

Bettie waved him silent and gestured the man to continue.

"I knew the family always celebrated their silly little Collins Day tonight so I wanted… I wanted someone to finally discover the truth, because, he keeps talking to me,"

Bettie hugged the man for some reason she didn't understand but she could tell that he wasn't a bad person, he was just a man that had been forced by a situation to react.

Granted Bettie never would have decided to live in the walls of a house if she was homeless, but she could understand if someone was desperate enough.

"I never meant to kill Mr Collins but he caught me and I hate living with that corpse anyway. Please arrest me. At least you guys have heating, meals and free water. You have any idea how annoying it is having to wake up in the middle of the night just to get a day's supply of water,"

Bettie smiled and shook her head as Graham cuffed the man and arrested him for murder.

"Why did you try to kill Tom? You must have seen where Mr Collins kept the illegal things we bought back from the Navy and programmed the nerve agent," Bettie said.

The man's smile deepened. "I never wanted to

kill Tom. I was aiming for Beatrice. I didn't know you needed to programme the nerve agent so that only means one thing, doesn't it Miss English?"

Bettie waved Graham so he took the man over to the nearest police car and Bettie was just shocked at yet another secret this family held. Mr Collins had programmed the nerve agent to kill Tom before he died, Bettie wasn't even sure she wanted to know why Mr Collins wanted to kill him (maybe he believed it was Tom who was having the affair with the wife) but Bettie knew one thing for sure.

She was really glad that the man, whoever he was, had invited her tonight so she could uncover the secrets, lies and deceptions that had been eating this family away for so long. And now, hopefully, just hopefully Beatrice could find some peace and move on from Collins Day.

And as Bettie went home to kiss her two little angels goodnight, she really hoped that was true. Because she had seen first-hand the sheer cost of people not being able to move on from the past.

It never ended well and it never led to a happy Christmas.

BETTIE PRIVATE INVESTIGATOR SHORT STORY
COLLECTION VOLUME 3

BODIES IN THE BOOT
5th October 2023
Medway, Kent, England

"How many bodies could you fit in there Auntie?"

Private eye Bettie English just laughed and grinned as she leant against the icy cold metal pillar at the car dealership she was visiting with her nephew Sean. She had to admit that the car dealership was rather nice considering this was Medway of all places, with its wide forecourt that wrapped around the main metal building perfectly.

There was a great range of cars on display, and Bettie couldn't have cared less about their names and models, because she was useless at cars. But there were plenty of red, black and blue cars in all different shapes and sizes in neat little rows on the forecourt.

Bettie sort of recognised some of the brands like Fiat, Citroen and Ford, but she had to smile to herself because she was useless at their models. They all just looked the same to her, a metal box on top of four wheels.

Bettie waved at a young man in the dealership's tight black uniform as he led a young couple followed by a first-time buyer round the forecourt. She had no idea why a first-time buyer was looking at cars at this end of the court. They were stupidly overpriced and Bettie was only up here because she had wanted to play a game with Sean.

The game was simple and Bettie couldn't deny it was great fun. Whenever her and Sean opened a car boot, they had to guess how many bodies they could fit inside.

Bettie had no idea how she was going to tell her Detective boyfriend, Graham Adams, later on but she knew she would and they would laugh about it.

Bettie went over to Sean and he definitely had great taste. He was looking at a small black car that would be hard to notice, it would fit in small gaps easily enough and it was probably quicker than it looked. Bettie wasn't sure if the price tag of £6,000 was right and she could afford that from a single hour of work but she wasn't buying it for Sean.

The entire point why Bettie had come with Sean to the dealership was to help him find a good car (not that she knew what she was looking for) and she wanted to teach him that even though she was a millionaire and him and his boyfriend lived with them. It never hurt to learn money lessons, which was why Sean had to buy this car with his own money.

"I'm thinking two bodies," Sean said grinning and running a hand through his longish blond hair with tastefully done pink highlights.

Bettie smiled and shook her head. He wasn't wrong, the black car did have a big boot but it wasn't big enough for two adult bodies inside. Maybe an adult and a dwarf but not two adults.

"Miss English?"

Bettie turned around and forced herself to smile as the head of the dealership came over with a massive frown on her face. The woman looked rather good in a dirty white blouse with tons of creases in it, her black trousers had holes in and her high heels looked like they were about to break at any moment.

"Are you the President of the British Private Eye Federation?" the woman asked.

Bettie nodded. She loved being the President of the Federation who oversaw all private investigators in the UK that allowed her to help innocent people, improve lives and she had the power equal to some small countries thanks to the Federation's blackmail files. Something she intended never ever to use.

"Yes I am," Bettie said. "Can I help you at all?"

The head of the dealership came closer and Bettie looked at her name tag, Cindy. Bettie wanted to cough as the sheer awful hints of fish, chips and fried food filled her senses. It was awful.

"I found a body of sorts in the boot of my car attached to a note that says I'm going to die in ten minutes,"

Bettie looked at Sean. As much as she wanted to keep looking for a new car, this was definitely going to have to wait. Cindy was in danger and Bettie couldn't let anything bad happen. And it would be good for business to (Cindy might even give them a free car out of it).

"I need to see your car," Bettie said.

"Of course," Cindy said. "Oh thank you, thank you Miss English,"

Bettie just grinned at Sean because she had a feeling that this case was going to be wonderfully weird, chaotic and very odd indeed.

***

A few moments later, Bettie frowned as Cindy opened the booth of her large silver Fiat in the back car park of the dealership. There was a high, thick green fence that ran along the sides of the car park, and you could only come through it by the forecourt and a small blue door that led into the main building.

Both required a passcode.

Bettie liked how Sean looked like he was playing on his phone, but he was probably already "hacking" into the dealership's security cameras. She loved having a postgraduate with her specialising in Advanced Technological Engineering, or a drone and computing degree as she liked to describe it.

"Here you go," Cindy said. "I hate this, I just hate this,"

Bettie gently rubbed Cindy's shoulder as she went closer to the boot. There was a large manakin inside without a face, features or any clothes on. But there was a handwritten note that had been taped to the face of the manakin.

Bettie wanted to focus on the note but she leant into the booth of the car for a moment. She carefully looked around the rusty trim of the boot, and checked for any fabric, fibres or anything else that might tell her who did this.

There was nothing.

The sound of customers laughing, making offers and bargaining made Bettie smile. She really hoped everyone here was getting a good deal for their cars and everything was working.

She had heard way too many horror stories of dealerships selling bad cars to too many innocent people. She really wanted everyone to get good cars here, it was the least the people of Medway deserved. Most people in this district could barely afford heating and food, let alone a new car.

Bettie put on her gloves that she always carried with her, and she read the note out to Sean.

"In ten minutes, I'm going to kill you, bury you and make you pay for what you're doing here," Bettie said.

Sean smiled. "Well, that would explain what I've found in your security logs and your computer systems?"

Bettie folded her arms and just looked at Cindy.

She knew something wasn't right here.

"You," Sean said, "have been coming to the forecourt at 2 am at night every Monday for the past four months. You log in and you've been changed financial records to increase the interest people are paying after they've already signed the contracts,"

Cindy leant against her car. "You have no right to hack into my systems. That's a crime,"

"I could call my detective boyfriend and see what he has to say about this," Bettie said.

Sean took a step closer to Cindy. "Even worse, you keep digital records of all the faults in your cars, but the paperwork you give to buyers say they are perfectly in order,"

Bettie really hated Cindy. How the hell could she betray, hurt and con so many innocent people that only wanted a cheaper car instead of going to a franchise of a major brand. It was disgusting.

"My death threat though," Cindy said.

Bettie nodded. "We'll investigate that but I promise you there will be a price to pay for your criminal activities,"

Cindy shook her head. "Just find out who wants to kill me,"

Bettie was about to say something but Cindy just walked off, so Bettie focused on the note and noticed it had been written on the dealership's own branded paper.

"You know someone here wants revenge," Bettie

said. "Cross-reference all the employees and their families with any purchases in the last, two years,"

"Okay," Sean said.

Bettie went over to the thick green security fence that separated the forecourt from the secured parking area. The small silver pad was perfectly clean with no marks, fingerprints or signs it had been interfered with.

Bettie was sure it was an employee of the dealership and that only confirmed her theory even more. If an outsider had done this then there would be signs of someone trying to break in.

"No signs of anyone coming or going on the security footage, but I think it was looped round so it wasn't really recording. It isn't even picking us up now," Sean said.

Bettie really liked having Sean with her. He was always a brilliant crime-solving partner. She felt lucky to have him in her life, unlike his mother.

"Anything on the purchases?"

"Still cross-referencing,"

Bettie nodded and she headed over to the blue door on the other side of the secure parking area and went inside the main building. She needed to talk to someone and she needed to get to the bottom of this threat before a woman died.

Cindy might not have been innocent but she never ever deserved to die.

***

"You could fit tons of bodies in that car," Sean

said grinning.

Bettie laughed as she stood in the middle of the beautiful showroom in the main building, and she was shocked at how great it looked. The grey tile flooring was shiny, sterile and Bettie was slightly pleased to see she had lost most of her baby weight (at last) in her reflection.

There were eight posh, expensive BMWs, Land Rovers and a lot more expensive cars she didn't recognise, lined up against the floor-to-ceiling windows facing the forecourt, and the small offices looked impressive behind the glass wall behind her.

Bettie had no idea how the hell people were meant to afford the BMWs, Land Rovers and other cars, but this dealership clearly had ambition.

And Bettie couldn't deny Sean wasn't wrong about the boot of the Land Rover. A killer could probably fit tons of bodies inside, something she hoped would never ever be tested.

"Can I help you?" a middle-aged man asked.

Bettie was glad her plan had finally worked. Being President of the Federation had always meant she had needed to look imposing, scary and powerful time to time, and apparently she had the *look* down perfectly these days. So she could activate it whenever she wanted.

And con artists, like this dealership, always liked money and power.

"We're looking for a car for my nephew and I'm

wondering what would you recommend," Bettie said. "Can we talk in your office?"

Bettie noticed the middle-aged man's name tag said Carl, and he was a step down from Cindy. Maybe he wanted to kill her to take over.

"No, I'm afraid some trainees are in my office at the moment," Carl said gesturing behind him where there were five trainees watching someone on a computer.

Bettie hadn't realised there might be trainees here, and there was a chance that someone might have gotten a job as a trainee to target the dealership. They wouldn't pop up on the main employees list because they were "only" a trainee.

"Um," Sean said clearly making the same connection, "how many trainees do you have at the moment? I have a friend that might want a job,"

Carl's face lit up. "Oh that is wonderful. We always need more trainees and we have a lot of great benefits, but I'm afraid we're fully booked at the moment with trainees. We only have eight spaces you see,"

Bettie cocked her head. That didn't make any sense, because there were only five trainees behind the computer and she couldn't see any more in the showroom.

Bettie went over to the massive floor-to-ceiling windows and noticed only one trainee outside showing people round the cars.

"Where are the other two trainees?" Bettie asked.

Carl shrugged. "I don't know. They are all meant to be here,"

Bettie checked her watch and bit her lower lip. It was probably already past the ten-minute mark, so they might already be too late.

"I need you to find them now," Bettie said.

"Who the hell do you think you are bossing me about?" Carl asked.

"I am Private Eye Bettie English, President of the British Private Eye Federation and unless you want your boss to die you will help me,"

Carl stumbled back a little like Bettie had actually hit him or something. Bettie just glared at him and Carl hurried off.

"Should we look ourselves?" Sean asked.

Bettie shook her head. Something wasn't right here. Clearly the dealership was ripping people off, changing interest payments after contracts were signed and selling bad cars as good ones. That made sense, and as much as Bettie didn't want to admit it that was normal in the dealership game.

But why the manakin?

Bettie couldn't understand why use the manakin in the car boot to scare Cindy or warn her. It made no sense because if the trainee or whoever really was going to kill Cindy then why not just kill her?

Unless Cindy was never meant to die and she had set up this plan in the first place.

"Where's Cindy's office? Did you see it on the

security footage?"

Sean led Bettie across the showroom and into a large corner with more desks, chairs and cabinets than Bettie had ever seen before. The entire office smelt of coffee, chips and fried fish, which made Bettie really want to vomit. It was so overwhelming.

Bettie went over to the perfectly arranged desk and found a notepad that Cindy had been writing on. Then she compared the writing on the notepad to the note on the manakin.

It was a match.

"Why do this?" Bettie asked. "Why would Cindy want us to investigate and why would she threaten herself?"

Carl came into the office. "I've found the two trainees, they were making out in the toilets. Typical young men and women,"

Bettie was glad that loose thread was dealt with, so Cindy was clearly up to something but she had no idea what.

"Carl," Bettie said, "why would Cindy threaten herself?"

"Bloody bastard," Carl said. "She's going to abandon ship and leave me for the cops. I knew it was wrong, it was bloody stupid but I needed the money,"

Bettie leant across the desk. "If you want any chance of not going to prison then you need to tell me everything,"

"Auntie," Sean said taking out his phone, "cross-referencing came back and every single current and former employee was forced to buy a car and they are still paying it off,"

Bettie couldn't believe that. That was outrageous and extremely illegal, and that was just messed up.

"Talk," Bettie said.

"Fine, me and Cindy started this dealership after university because we wanted some fun, we wanted a business and we used to steal cars for a living. It wasn't hard to fake reports and MOTs,"

Bettie rolled her eyes. She really didn't like these people.

"Then we realised running a business is a little hard so we got more and more employees. But when we had to cut their wages, they threatened to leave so Cindy offered them a *discount* on a car,"

"And," Bettie said, "that's when you nailed them because they brought the car on finance and then you changed the interest rates so much you trapped them. What was the deal Carl? If they keep working and shut their mouths, you do it interest-free?"

Carl nodded and looked to the ground.

"What changed?" Sean asked.

"One of the trainees who brought a car off us was outraged, she spoke up and went to the cops. We increased her interest rates to crippling amounts so she didn't retract her statement from the cops,"

Bettie clicked her fingers. There was something on the local news (the only thing that seemed to make her baby boy sleep at the moment) about this. A 19-year-old woman had died in a drunk car crash last week, she had been drinking and upset over crippling interest repayments.

"You killed that woman," Bettie said. "You might not have crashed the car but she wouldn't have been drinking if you hadn't done that,"

Carl shrugged. "Business is business,"

Bettie just looked at Sean. She hated these people and she was going to make them pay, and Bettie was going to do everything in her power to give the victims of this con their money back.

Bettie went round the desk and got very close to Carl's ear.

"So the cops are coming here and Cindy has probably run. I have the power and influence to get you a reduced prison sentence but you have to come clean about your operation,"

"I can't," Carl said. "Cindy will ruin me,"

Bettie laughed. "Then you have clearly never met the Federation. You are conning tons of innocent people and you caused a young woman to die. If you don't do the right thing then I will use the Federation's resources to bury you alive,"

Bettie forced herself not to frown as she stood up. She hated being like this but she hated people like Carl and Cindy even more. It was just unforgivable to take advantage of so many innocent, good people that only wanted a damn car to get to work.

"She does have the power to do it," Sean said.

"Especially with the evidence I've found,"

Carl stood up and paced round the office for a few moments. Bettie really hoped he was going to make the right choice.

"Fine," Carl said. "I'll testify to everything that happened here and I'll even tell you where Cindy probably is. Just don't… send me to jail,"

Bettie laughed because Cindy was finally going to get justice and she actually had an idea about what to do with dear old Carl.

***

A few hours later, Bettie leant against an awfully cold metal pillar in the forecourt of the dealership, and she just smiled at all the flashing red and blue lights of the four police cars that blocked the road entrance inside. There weren't any cars left on the forecourt and Bettie was surprised to see so many weeds had cracked the concrete under the cars.

Apparently all of them had been stolen from one place or another, and her sexy, wonderful boyfriend Graham had confirmed the dealership had been running this scam for about two decades. Cindy wasn't even as young as she looked.

Bettie watched as one of the police cars drove away with Carl and some of the other employees in the back. She didn't feel sorry for Graham or the other detectives that were going to have to sort this mess out. Thankfully, she would send off all the evidence they had collected in a moment, so hopefully that would allow the detectives to get home to their families sooner.

A small group of young men and women in hoodies and black jogging bottoms were gathered just at the road entrance. Bettie didn't like how sad, hopeless and disappointed they looked because they had all probably brought cars here at one point or another. And they had probably figured it out that they were conned.

So a ton of their money was wasted at a time when no one could really afford it.

Bettie waved as Graham, in his sexy white shirt and trousers, and Sean came over after opening the main building's door for a bunch of uniform officers to carry out boxes of paperwork.

The cold night air smelt of strong bitter coffee, fried fish and chips and Bettie was so looking forward to going home to her two sweet twins. Then she was going to go for a shower, she really didn't want to smell of fish and chips anymore, the damn smell had probably soaked into her clothes.

"My officers picked up Cindy a few minutes ago trying to flee to Dover," Graham said. "She's silent but there are records and laptops in her boot. We'll nail her for this fraud,"

"Thank you," Bettie said blowing the man she loved a kiss. "What's going to happen to Carl and the others?"

Graham shrugged. "That's up for the Crown Prosecution Service to decide. Carl was a big player but testifying will help him, and the others were only victims in truth so we only need a statement,"

"Good," Sean said playing with some brand-new car keys in his hands.

"You didn't," Graham said playfully hitting Bettie's arm.

"Well, it isn't my fault they left the car keys unattended and their computers open," Bettie said. "As a private eye, I only care about solving crimes, helping people and benefiting my business,"

"I so did not hear that," Graham said before giving Bettie a kiss on the cheek and going over to some uniformed officers.

Sean folded his arms and grinned. "What are you going to do about the victims?"

Bettie smiled. "Oh you know, what's the point of being a millionaire if you can't help people? All the victims will suddenly and mysteriously be sent £10,000 tomorrow afternoon with a small note,"

"Mysteriously, sure," Sean said hugging Bettie. "I love you Auntie,"

"I love you too Sean,"

Bettie followed Sean over to the other side of the secure parking area, and there was only one car left a massive black Land Rover and Bettie was seriously impressed. That would be a great car for a high-speed chase.

"Open the boot," Sean said climbing into the front seat.

Bettie popped up the boot and gasped as ten manakins popped out from under a big blue blanket.

Bettie just laughed and laughed and she really did love her nephew, and at least the age-old question was answered. How many bodies could you fit in there, and Bettie had to admit she loved being a private eye, an auntie and a girlfriend to a detective a lot more than she ever wanted to admit.

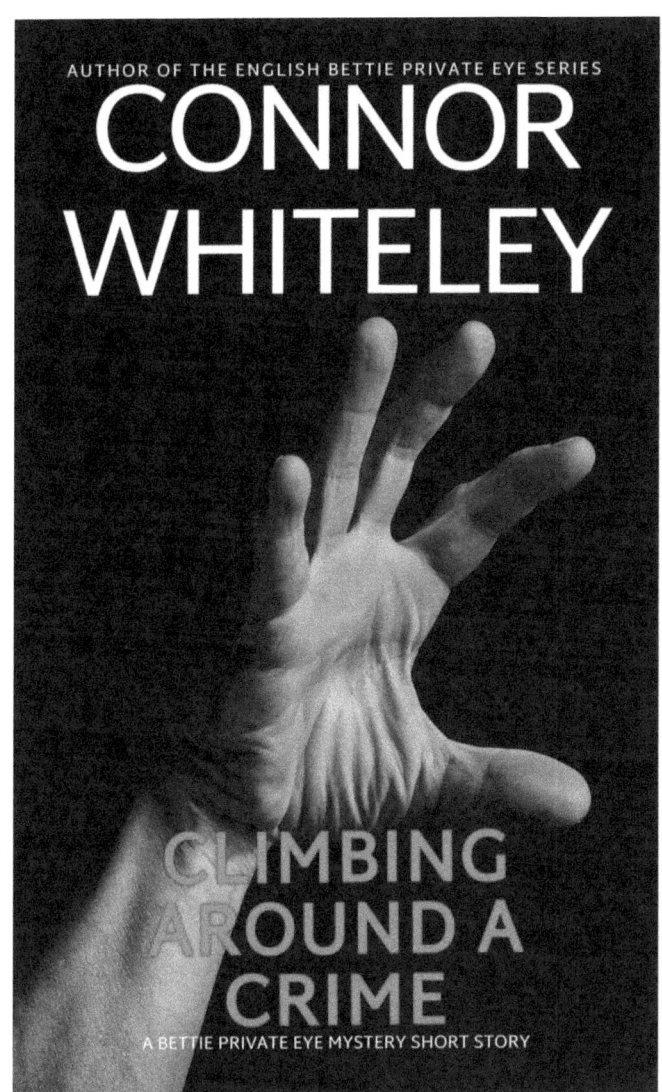

CLIMBING AROUND A CRIME

Of all the ways private eye Bettie English had wanted to spend her Friday evening when her best friend and personal assistant Fran had suggested they have some "fun", Bettie certainly hadn't expected to be doing bouldering of all things.

Bettie was a good ten metres up in the air and barely clinging to the purple handholds that pretended to look like rocks. There were only a few millimetres of the handhold for her to actually hold onto and even she had to admit, she might have pushed herself a little too far this time.

She had already been climbing for over an hour in the massive bouldering centre. A large grey warehouse-like building with fake wooden rock-like walls covered in orange, grey and purple handholds with each of them being a different difficulty.

Bettie had wanted to try the red, blue and white handholds but she wasn't crazy enough to try them. They were way too hard and her arms, legs and bum ached.

It had been ages since she had done "this" type of exercise that required such a firm grip that she couldn't train herself by chasing bad guys, defending herself from criminals and doing her normal cardio.

Bettie hissed a little as her fingers grew more and more tired and she could see the next purple handhold a little further up from her. She could reach it, she knew she could and she was determined to do it.

Bettie wasn't exactly a fan of the gentle hip-pop music playing in the background but a lot of other people clearly liked it as they laughed, talked and planned their next climb with each other.

She looked over to her left and there was a short little kid, maybe twelve, just shooting up a red handhold route without a sweat. When her two beautiful twins were old enough, she was so bringing them here.

Bettie hissed as she realised bouldering required weird hand strength that she seriously didn't have, but she loved it anyway. It was so much fun climbing up the handholds, stretching herself and proving that she was a strong independent woman that could do anything she put her mind to.

Except she could feel her fingers were about to give out on her.

She fell.

Bettie landed straight down on the soft, spongy

grey floor below and she laughed to herself. She had always liked falling and this had been a great idea of Fran's to come here after work.

"Are you okay?" Fran asked.

Bettie got up and laughed at she looked as her best friend, smiling and wearing her black gym top and activewear jogging bottoms. Apparently, Fran did this a lot but Bettie was rather impressed she was doing a lot better than her friend on her first time.

"I'm going to start myself off again on a grey route," Fran said going over to the climbing wall.

Bettie nodded. She couldn't blame Fran at all for wanting to take the easiest route, her fingers and arms were killing her but that was all part of the fun.

Someone screamed.

Bettie spun and gasped as she saw a young woman fall twelve metres through the air with two handholds flying off the wall.

The woman landed with a thud and Bettie rushed over.

She knocked people out the way as she rushed over the other side of the centre. She even leapt over a small child.

A group of other people were already surrounding the young woman and Bettie just pushed past them.

"Who are you?" someone asked in Adidas sportswear.

"Bettie English, private eye," she said kneeling down next to the young woman.

Bettie was surprised at the sheer sponginess of the floor as she knelt down next to the young woman who was hissing in pain, holding her ankle and her black, tight sportswear was hugging her slim body.

Bettie wasn't exactly a fan of how all the men and women at the centre crowded around her like they were trying to suffocate her, but they were asking questions and trying to help.

The worst of it was the awful hints of sweat, sweat and more sweat that filled the centre. Bettie didn't mind it too much but she was looking forward to getting some fresh air later on, but right now she just needed to help this young woman.

"What happened?" Bettie asked as calmly and reassuringly as she could.

The young woman held onto Bettie's hand. "I was climbing like I've done a thousand times and the handholds just gave way. They spin rarely but never fall off,"

"Excuse me. Excuse me," a man said as he pushed himself through the crowd.

Bettie rubbed the woman's hand gently before she stood up and let the man in his first-aid uniform take over.

She went out of the crowd and enjoyed the slightly less intensely sweaty air, and then she went over to Fran who was taking photos of the handholds.

Bettie knelt down next to them and Fran

followed. She had liked it how resourceful, clever and focused Fran was. Fran had probably already sent the photos to the Federation for some kind of analysis that Bettie didn't want to focus on right now.

"Here," Bettie said pointing to the handholds. "The attachments to the walls have been cut,"

Bettie hated seeing the perfectly smooth almost saw-like markings on the handholds. And Bettie wouldn't have been surprised if someone had tried to kill or hurt the young woman on purpose.

"How long have you been coming here?" Bettie asked Fran.

"Maybe four months," Fran said looking over at the young woman. "Bethany was here before I started and she's a competitive one. She represents Kent at national competitions. She's really nice too,"

Bettie nodded. She had heard of national contests for all sorts of weird and wonderful sports but bouldering just seemed a little too niche.

"How many of the people here are competitive?" Bettie asked standing up.

"Most of them actually. There's a set of trials coming up and everyone has to requalify or get in for the first time,"

"Show me the person who might do this," Bettie said not knowing if Fran was observant enough to guess who might be responsible.

A few moments later, the crowd surrounding Bethany broke apart and the man in the first aid uniform carefully walked next to her as she went across the centre to the reception area. Bettie was glad she seemed okay and nothing was broken, so hopefully she had "only" sprained her ankle.

But for the sake of Bethany and the others at the centre, Bettie wasn't leaving until she found out who could have done this.

"Lukas," Fran said.

Bettie smiled as a very fit man in his early thirties came over topless showing off his massive biceps and six-pack, and long brown hair. He winked at Bettie and she just frowned.

"It's a shame about Beth, right?" Lukas asked. "I told her, she gonna be more careful,"

Bettie smiled. "You almost sound like you wanted this to happen,"

Lukas pointed a warning finger at Bettie. "No. Beth is the only one that climbs that route tonight, she practises all tonight doing the exact same route because it's one of the hardest here. All of us have to train on lesser routes,"

Bettie tried to remember how long Beth had been here before or after them. Beth had turned up about the same time as them so she had been doing the route for about an hour before it broke.

That didn't make any sense.

"Do you know how to damage these handholds enough?" Bettie asked.

"No, no one does except Mike, the manager. I come here to train, socialise and become good enough to compete. That is it and I do not waste my time on pretenders like Beth. Now if you excuse me, I have training to do,"

Bettie folded her arms as Lukas went away and the idiot turned round to flex a little for her. It wasn't a bad sight but she hated guys like that.

"He isn't wrong Bet," Fran said gesturing they should go to the reception area.

Bettie followed Fran as the two of them went across the spongy floor with the hints of sweat, manly musk and chalk filling the air.

"I know," Bettie said. "I have little idea how someone could change and damage the handholds so easily. Considering this has been open all day and I presume other people have used the route,"

"I'll get the camera footage,"

"Thank you," Bettie said.

Bettie stepped out the way of a small child as he leapt off one of the walls and almost took her out.

"I'm so sorry," his mother said.

"It's fine. Your son's great at climbing," Bettie said.

She went over to the reception area which was nothing more than a large front desk, a row of black metal tables and some horrible black chairs that Bettie seriously didn't want to sit in. They just looked plain uncomfortable.

Bettie waved at Beth as she was sitting on one of the horrible chairs with an ice pack on her ankle, and she was playing on her phone.

"Some people call you a pretender," Bettie said.

"Ha," Bethany said. "Lukas and the other guys just can't accept that I qualified for nationals every year since I was 18. I'm good at bouldering, I work hard and I make sure other people benefit from my work,"

Bettie leant on the back of a chair. "How do other people benefit?"

"This centre. A few years ago, it needed to up its membership cost to keep its doors open, and every April it wants to increase its costs. I donate a few tens of thousands to keep prices down,"

Bettie was amazed. That was brilliant of Bethany and she had no idea there was that much money in bouldering competitions that she could afford to donate like that.

"I live off my day job and my competition money pays for very nice holidays with my boyfriend," Bethany said. "And this place was where I fell in love with bouldering, so why shouldn't others have the same chance?"

Bettie nodded. That was a great point but maybe that was what had annoyed someone enough to attack her tonight. She had learnt over the years with her own extreme acts of charity (the benefits of being a millionaire) that it always annoyed certain organisations and people more than they ever wanted to admit.

"Thank you for your time," Bettie said going

back over to Fran.

"At least six other people have used that same route today. No accidents, no problems, no time to damage the handholds," Fran said closing her phone.

Bettie shook her head. It was worth a shot but that would have been too easy.

"I presume you got the Federation to run background checks on Bethany," Bettie said.

"I am offended you needed to ask Bet,"

Bettie laughed as she waved over a large man with the nametag "Mike."

"Everything checks out with Bethany," Fran said. "No problems, no money issues and she is basically keeping this place afloat,"

"Find out everything you can about rival businesses and people that want to see this place shut,"

Bettie nodded her thanks to Fran as she went over to Bethany and sat down. Fran's face twisted into a mixture of pain and just being uncomfortable as she sat down.

"Miss English," Mike said, "it is a pleasure to have you here tonight. I presume you're working to find out what happened to Bethany?"

"I am," Bettie said gesturing to the other people bouldering. "Do you think any of them could have done it?"

"God no," Mike said. "It isn't possible because these are all good people and everyone knows that Beth is keeping this place open. It's public knowledge and we all owe Beth a great debt,"

"Does anyone not like you being open?"

Mike rolled his eyes. "My wife. No, I'm joking. Maybe Lukas because his father wanted to redevelop this site and expand the centre so we do other sports as well,"

Bettie looked at Lukas at the very top of the bouldering wall after completing the blue and white route, which was meant to be the hardest one. He was skilled, he didn't like Bethany but she just wasn't sure he could damage the handholds.

"Help!" Fran shouted.

Bettie spun around.

Bethany was coughing and gasping and winded.

She collapsed to the ground.

Bettie rushed over.

She slammed an open hand on Beth's back.

Something flew out of Beth's mouth and she gasped in as much air as she possibly could.

Bettie knelt on the ground and inspected the small chunk of chalk that had shot out of Bethany's mouth. It was small and neatly cut, this wasn't something someone had quickly broken off. Someone had planned this carefully and purposefully.

Then Bettie noticed Beth had a small plate of energy balls in front of her. And she realised someone really wanted Bethany well and truly gone from this competition.

She went over to Beth's plate and broke up some

of the remaining energy balls and shook her head. All of them contained chunks of chalk designed to choke Beth.

Bettie looked at Mike. "Who the hell made these?"

He shrugged. "I don't know. I normally make them from scratch just for Beth. Not tonight though, not after the fall,"

"Fran, did you see anyone?"

"No sorry. I was deep diving on my phone,"

Bettie so badly wanted to roll her eyes, but Fran was just doing her job and Bettie couldn't moan at her for that. And she supposed it was slightly her fault too, she had just never expected someone to try and kill her again so soon.

"No," Bethany said. "You did make these for me,"

Bettie folded her arms, because something wasn't adding up here.

"I was talking to Miss English, I couldn't have given them to you," Mike said. "And you keep this place afloat, why would I want to kill you?"

Bettie clicked her fingers and smiled. This was all starting to make sense because Mike had probably owned this centre for more years than she wanted to think about, he had trained and had great athletes train here like Beth. She would have been surprised if there was anything he didn't know about bouldering.

Including the handholds.

And Bettie was willing to bet if she had a

Federation-approved lab test the handholds there would be some kind of substance, maybe glue, on the handholds that would have lasted until tonight. So only Beth could would have been affected.

"What did you study at university?" Bettie asked Mike.

"Chemistry,"

Bettie laughed. "Chemistry students would know about chemicals, substances and bonding strengths. How long did the handholds have to last until Beth came?"

Mike took a few steps back.

"And actually," Bettie said, "it didn't matter if you got one of the other staff members to give her the energy balls. You had already made them and why would your own staff assume you wanted to kill her?"

Mike took a few more steps back. Bettie and Fran followed him onto the spongy floor.

"Here it is," Fran said. "Two years ago your wife filed for divorce and retracted it at the same time as a massive gym company made you an offer to sell the centre,"

Bettie placed her hands on her hips. "But you couldn't sell and save face with Bethany giving you money. As you said, this centre is great because you've trained hard-working people. You couldn't shut down easily just because of a buyout,"

Bettie smiled as everyone had stopped bouldering now and everyone was starting to gather around Mike to stop him from escaping. But there was a large patch of bouldering wall exposed with a purple route.

Bettie seriously hoped he didn't climb up there to escape (not that there was anywhere to go).

"So what?" Fran asked. "Why try to kill Beth now?"

Bettie just shook her head at Mike. "The gym group has remade their offer haven't they? Your wife wants you home more and you want to get rid of this place and you want to save face. You can't have everything,"

"Traitor," Lukas said. "How dare you want to sell this place. The heart of our community. We trusted you,"

Bettie bit her lower lip as she realised just how seriously people took bouldering and now she truly focused on their postures, their manners and when all the men and women looked up, she noticed the truth.

Most of these were university students, bankers and office workers. Most of them had high-stress, intense jobs so this was their escape and this was their chance to relax and have fun with friends.

If this place went, then so many amazing benefits would be lost for them too.

"I wasn't trying to kill her," Mike said. "I only wanted to stop her competing so the money would dry up,"

Bettie went towards Mike and Mike just ran for the bouldering wall.

Bettie followed him.

Mike shot up the purple route.

Bettie didn't think. She only reacted. She climbed up the wall as fast as she could.

Mike was already at the top.

Bettie hissed as she climbed up. Her fingers and legs ached. Her forearms flooded with pain.

Her fingers felt like they were going to let go. She kept on climbing.

Everyone was cheering Bettie on and she just grinned as she climbed harder and harder.

She moved one hand at a time behind Mike and then she grabbed Mike's ankle and she leapt off the wall.

Mike screamed and Bettie laughed as the two of them fell to the ground and then Bettie climbed on top of Mike and pinned his arms behind his back.

"Fran," Bettie said, "please call Graham. I have a little gift for him,"

And as Fran went away to call Detective Graham Adams, Bettie just grinned at the chance to see her wonderful, sexy boyfriend again.

At least she had a hell of a story for him.

***

About two hours later, Bettie held sweet, cute baby Harrison in an adorable black puffer jacket outside of the centre surrounded by the bright red and blue flashing lights of three police cars. Bettie was rather impressed the police cars could fit inside the little car park that could barely fit ten cars inside, but they managed it.

The night was icy cold and Bettie was really enjoying the aromas of damp, strong bitter coffee and chocolate coming from the energy ball Fran was devouring next to her. It was so much better than the awful hints of sweat that had filled the bouldering centre.

Bettie loved how Graham was holding Elizabeth as she slept in his arms whilst he spoke to some uniformed cops about bagging and tagging the evidence and interviewing everyone. She had already passed her evidence over to him and he had mockingly hit her on the arm.

Apparently, Graham couldn't trust her to go anywhere without getting involved in a crime in one way or another. And Bettie couldn't really disagree but she loved her job, she loved helping people and she loved putting bad people away even more.

"Thank you," Graham said to the uniformed officers before coming over to Bettie and Fran. "Bethany's going to make a full recovery before the tryouts,"

"Good," Bettie said as she bounced Harrison a little.

"Mummy," Harrison said pointing to the energy ball in Fran's hand.

"No, sweetheart you can't have nuts until you're older,"

Harrison just buried his face in her neck and Bettie kissed him lightly on the head. She really did love her kids.

"What's going to happen to this place now?" Graham asked. "The owner's been arrested, Beth probably won't want to keep funding it and I don't like how the gym company's going to buy it,"

Bettie just grinned and hugged little Harrison even tighter. She had absolutely no intention of allowing the gym company to buy the bouldering centre, shut it down and convert it into something new.

The local community needed the bouldering centre to destress, have fun and socialise after a hard day's work, or just to have fun.

"Fran," Bettie said grinning.

Fran took out her phone and showed Graham something.

"The British Private Eye Federation," Graham said clearly reading from something, "strongly believes in supporting businesses critical to the local community,"

Bettie nodded, because it was why she did what she did. She solved crime, helped people and improved lives.

"You're buying the centre and who's running it?" Graham asked.

"Once the paperwork goes through privately so the gym group will never have a chance to outbid us," Bettie said. "Someone from the Federation will manage it until Bethany has retired from competitions. Then she has agreed to run it on our behalf,"

"I love you," Graham said kissing Bettie on the lips.

Bettie seriously loved the feeling of his soft, beautiful lips against her.

And as Bettie and Fran took the twins home and left Graham to do what he did best as a cop, Bettie felt amazing because she had done a lot of good today. She had saved a life, stopped a man from graduating to murder and she had saved a business critical to the local community.

If that wasn't something to celebrate then Bettie seriously didn't want to know what was, and it was only possible because she had been climbing around a crime.

DAY TO REMEMBER
20th November 2023
London, England

She was about to have the most chilling phone call of her life.

"Just have a coffee already,"

As much as Private Eye Bettie English really liked her personal assistant Fran because she was kind, helpful and an amazing assistant that basically oversaw the day-to-day running of the British Private Eye Federation, so Bettie could focus on helping people and solving cases, Bettie just had to admit Fran was being a nightmare today.

Bettie had never really liked coming into her massive, executive office at the Federation's headquarters in London. Sure, she loved the massive floor-to-ceiling windows that allowed her to see all over London, and its immensely impressive skyline. She had always liked to watch the little white boats on the Thames, watch people coming and going in from the Houses of Parliament and see the happy tourists walking about below.

But the office just wasn't her home, or even where she liked to work.

Bettie wanted to be out on the streets, in the community and talking to the amazing people that her and her fellow private investigators helped every day. She seriously loved being President of the Federation but not when she had to give speeches.

"Do you want a coffee?" Fran asked.

Bettie just looked at Fran across her massive black glass desk with her three computer screens to one side, her laptop open with her emails and a small plate of Danish pastries.

Bettie would have preferred if Fran had gotten the pastries from a small local business instead of a major international corporation, but Fran had been in a rush apparently.

But Bettie couldn't deny the pastries smelt great with hints of vanilla, sugar and sweet strawberries filling the office. She could almost taste those wonderful strawberries on her tongue, but she wasn't going to give in to temptation just yet. She had a speech to write.

And she was really hoping something was going to pop up in the meantime to stop her.

"No, thank you," Bettie said. "I don't want a coffee. I want to get this speech done,"

"Why are you even doing a speech on Pro-

Transgender Healthcare? We all support trans people but we're private investigators, not politicians or doctors?" Fran asked.

Bettie smiled as she heard the muttering and shouting of people walking outside her office.

That was actually the question Bettie had been wondering herself. She had only been talking to her wonderful nephew, Sean, and his boyfriend last month about the awful state of transgender rights and healthcare in the UK. She completely agreed it needed to improve and these great people needed to be supported.

But she couldn't remember the exact moment where she had signed up to give a major keynote at a medical convention later on tonight.

Thankfully, she had six hours left.

Bettie just knew that wouldn't be enough time to write something worthy on the topic, considering how many lives and livelihoods it could affect.

She was the President of the Federation, her words had power. She could influence people positively or damn entire communities. That was a hell of a burden.

Bettie's phone rang.

Fran went to grab it from the desk but Bettie grabbed it first and answered.

"Miss English, is that you?" a man's voice said on the phone.

"Yes, who is this?" Bettie asked.

"I'm sorry for the call but you don't know me. I

got your name and number from Percy Munchin, he said if I was ever in trouble you would help me,"

As soon as the caller said Percy's name, Bettie just grinned. She hadn't heard from Percy for years but he was a great man, a brilliant speaker and one of the kindest men Bettie had ever had the privilege of meeting. Granted she had thought he was a serial killer for a few days but after that business was sorted out, he was delightful.

"Yes, I can help you. I think," Bettie said gesturing Fran to run a trace on the call.

"Percy also said you would trace the call and try to work out who I was. I'll save you the trouble. My name is Penelope Gray and me and my friends need your help because someone is threatening to kill us all tonight,"

Bettie gasped and nodded at Fran.

The voice, the chosen name of Penelope and the fact it was the 20th November made Bettie realise instantly that these death threats had to be connected to what today was for the trans community. Transgender Day of Remembrance was today, a chance for everyone in the world to remember, honour and want to support all the trans people that had been murdered in the last year for the simple reason of wanting to be themselves.

Bettie had stopped checking the numbers a few years back because the number of murders only increased year on year.

It was disgusting but Bettie had a chance to save lives and she fully intended to take it no matter how heartbreaking the situation might be.

"I'll be there immediately," Bettie said hanging up as Fran finished the trace.

***

20th November 2023

Canterbury, England

One thing Bettie did love about being President of the Federation was the UK Government allowed it to have its own array of vehicles with blue flashing lights, it meant she never had to wait in traffic. She loved that little detail.

As the massive black SUV she was in the back of started to drive into Canterbury, Bettie smiled as she was home. She liked seeing the thick oak, pine and silver birch trees lining the exit off the motorway. And in the distance, the impressive flint city wall that dated back to Roman times stood proudly.

Bettie couldn't wait to go home later on and see her boyfriend Graham, two beautiful kids and Sean. No doubt he would love her even more for helping out innocent trans people on today of all days.

As much as Bettie wanted to focus on her speech, something she had barely started writing on the way here, she just wanted to save the lives of these innocent people. She wouldn't allow another person to die, especially on a day that was meant to be about remembering the murdered.

Not adding to that evil tally.

She settled back in the soft, wonderfully warm car seat as Fran passed over an iPad with photos. Bettie was surprised by the slight coldness of the iPad but she took it.

Bettie couldn't believe how disgusting the images were. They were all photos of the outside of a local church with red paint, animal blood and anti-trans comments painted on the cream-bricked walls of the church.

Bettie felt her stomach tighten as she read the warnings, the death threats and all the disgusting stuff the attackers were saying. She just couldn't believe that people in the 21st century could be so foul to other people just because politicians and bigots said this was okay.

It was disgusting.

"We'll be there in a minute Madame President," John said from the front of the SUV.

Bettie just nodded. She had always liked John as her new head of security. She didn't think she needed John for a slight second, but she wanted to keep beautiful Graham happy after a massive assassination attempt (more like attempt*s*) were made on her a few months ago.

"What did the police say?" Bettie asked passing the iPad back to Fran.

"Nothing. Simple case of vandalising and this is not the job of the police where there are more important cases to investigate," Fran said.

Bettie laughed. "Let me guess, the police aren't interested in actionable death threats made against trans people,"

"Of course not," Fran said.

Bettie shook her head as the SUV pulled to a stop and John opened the door for Bettie.

She got out and shivered a little and pulled her thick black trench coat around tighter. She wasn't exactly a fan of the small square car park they were in, but she supposed John would have liked it with its thick tree cover, high brick walls covered in death threats and no one else was about.

Even though Bettie really didn't like the cracked roof tiles and the plastic pipes hanging off the roofs of the surrounding, almost abandoned former council houses.

Of the few windows Bettie could see behind the tall walls, they all looked cracked, cold and ugly. Bettie had a bad feeling about this.

Something just felt off.

The rich aroma of curries, spices and crispy bacon filled the air and Bettie was so tempted to find whatever restaurant that was coming from. Then she laughed as Fran brought over a small box of Danish pastries and ate one.

"I'm not leaving these behind," Fran said.

"Fair enough," Bettie said smiling before turning to a very tall woman coming towards them.

Bettie had to admit Penelope was an impressive woman with her long brown hair, slim body and tight black peacoat that highlighted her feminine body really well.

"I like your coat, it's great," Bettie said trying to be as supportive and affirming as she could.

Penelope nodded her thanks and gestured to the death threats painted on the walls.

Bettie shook her head but these were different from the ones in the photos. There were brush marks, angles and even small pieces of fabric mixed into the paint here. The words were written too quickly and harshly to be readable but Bettie understood the general message.

This person wanted every single trans person to die in the world.

"I didn't send photos of these because, I don't know. We don't know who did these ones," Penelope said clearly trying to practise her voice training.

"Who did the photos you send us?" Bettie asked.

"Just some local kids. The children of the Priests of another church,"

"Why?" Fran asked coming closer. "And why would a trans group meet in a church? I thought the Church hated trans people,"

Penelope nodded. "On principle yes, but there are some churches that accept us and other queer people. This is a good one,"

Bettie looked at the massive church a few metres away from the car park, she wanted to force a smile. She couldn't. She just couldn't forgive churches and religion for what it had done to the queer community and her beautiful nephew.

Bettie went over to the rough writing Penelope was focusing on. She took a pair of blue crime-scene gloves that Fran gave her as she also came over.

"I have no idea who did this," Penelope said, "but I just don't want my friends to die,"

Bettie nodded as she knelt down and inspected the markings on the walls. The paint wasn't exactly dry and it was sticky and thick. It might not have been paint at all.

"Why do these idiots think you'll be easy pickings tonight?" Bettie asked after reading a line of hate.

Penelope frowned. "We have a Trans Day of Remembrance Service tonight in the Church. We'll be reading out over 390 names,"

"Jesus," Bettie said.

That was way too many dead people and Bettie hated it how her stomach twisted at the idea of the speech tonight.

Bettie shook the thought away and focused back on the hate writing in front of her. The ground was awfully cold and rough but Bettie ran a finger over the writing and a red sticky substance came off the wall.

"Fran," Bettie said, "is this fake blood from productions and film sets?"

"Definitely," Fran said. "My daughter uses this a lot in her productions. It's really cheap stuff but it's effective for budget movies,"

Bettie was really pleased Fran's daughter was finally getting the chance to produce her own indie films, and Fran was travelling to Venice next year to hopefully see her daughter get an award. Bettie couldn't have been more pleased for Fran.

"Why use false blood from film sets?" Penelope asked.

Bettie stood up and looked over at the walls of the church. Even from a small distance, Bettie could see the markings, writing and death threats were all different.

These definitely weren't done by the same person.

"Stop there!" John shouted.

Bettie froze and saw that John was pointing his small sidearm (something Bettie forgot he had) at a young man walking into the car park.

He was focused on Penelope, dressed in all-black and Bettie just knew he was here to hurt Penelope.

Something she wasn't going to allow.

"I said stop. I'm licensed to shoot," John said.

The SUV's horn went off.

Bettie looked around. There were more young men in all-black entering the car park.

Most were climbing over the walls.

"Stop!" Bettie shouted with as much authority as she could. "You will *not* harm her!"

The young men all stopped and Bettie couldn't tell them apart in their all-black clothing.

"He ain't a woman," the young man said that John was aiming at.

"He's an unholy slut. He ain't in the bible," another young man said.

Bettie also wanted to point out the bible said a person could be stoned for wearing two different types of fabric but this probably wasn't the time for bible lessons.

"She is a woman," Bettie said. "It is ridiculous that you have nothing better to do than attack people and threaten them,"

Bettie gestured to the vandalism on the wall behind her.

"We ain't do that bitch," another young man said.

Bettie was about to protest but she believed him. These were young men, clearly religious, and Penelope had said sons of priests had attacked the church.

Someone else was behind these focused death threats.

The young men charged.

John fired.

The bullet screamed through the air.

Hitting the man's leg.

He went down.

The other young men charged.

Bettie grabbed Penelope. Throwing her towards John.

John gripped her. Throwing Penelope into the

SUV.

Bettie charged forward.

Rushing towards the young men.

They stopped.

Bettie didn't.

She punched them.

Giving them a left-hook. Then right-hook. Then jabs to the stomach.

Two young men fell to the floor.

Bettie ducked.

A fist shot past her from behind.

Bettie spun around.

Punching another man in the balls.

He slammed to the ground.

Bettie stood up and just grinned as there were no more attackers around and Fran and Penelope were getting back out of the SUV.

"Madame President how am I meant to protect you if you don't get to cover?" John asked grinning.

Bettie shrugged as she went over to the young man that John had shot. She was more than glad not a lot of blood had come out of the wound and it seemed to be just a flesh wound.

Of course the young man was rolling about, acting like a big baby but Bettie placed her right boot on his chest and looked down at him.

His eyes opened and Bettie just smiled.

"I never like hurting people," Bettie said. "I hate it but this was self-defence,"

"I'll call an ambulance," Fran said, "and the police."

Bettie had no idea what the point of calling the police was. If her boyfriend Graham was still a cop then he could deal with this but some corrupt officials had made that option impossible.

"Why are you defending a bitch?" the young man asked.

Bettie took her boot off his chest and helped the young man up. She threw one of his arms round her shoulders and Bettie grabbed him by the waist.

"Look at her," Bettie said. "Actually look at Penelope, she isn't a monster, she isn't crazy. She's just a woman wanting to live a normal life,"

"He ain't a woman!"

Bettie took her arm off his waist and the young man struggled to stand so he fell back down to the ground and Bettie shivered a little as an icy cold breeze blew in the car park.

"Who did this?" Bettie asked. "You have to know something about this. You cannot be the only transphobe in Canterbury,"

The young man grinned.

Bettie went over to him and searched his pockets. He tried to protest but it wasn't hard to find his locked phone.

"Fran, I need the unlocker please?" Bettie asked.

A moment later Fran came off and passed Bettie a small USB stick-like device that Bettie held over the phone screen and a moment later she was in.

"That ain't legal," the young man said who turned out to be Charlie.

"I'm a private eye. I don't need to follow the law at times,"

Bettie wanted to add on how she would never follow the law if it meant saving lives but she didn't want to get Charlie fired up again.

Bettie went through his contacts and apps, and she found a strange social networking app called *TwoG*. Bettie rolled her eyes as soon as she clicked on it and the motto *there are only two genders* popped up on the screen.

A second later, Bettie was scrolling through thousands upon thousands of anti-trans messages. There were pictures of dead bodies, mutilated corpses and extremely transphobic memes.

Bettie shivered and closed the app. That was outrageous and sickening and just disgusting. Some of the pictures of dead trans people barely seemed to be 18.

She just looked at Charlie and she took a deep breath of the rich curry-scented air. It barely calmed her down enough not to kick him in the nuts.

It was the least he deserved.

Fran took Charlie's phone, gasped and then looked like she was doing some techy stuff to do it with more advance gadgets the Federation had access to.

The loud beep of sirens filled the air as two

ambulances and two police cars came into the car park. Bettie just rolled her eyes. This wasn't what she needed.

Two police constables came out with handcuffs and started to walk towards Bettie, but Bettie just showed them her Federation ID, the constables sighed and went off to the real criminals that were still rolling and screaming about on the floor.

She was more than glad the police were too scared to arrest Federation members at times.

"Bet," Fran said coming over as paramedics dealt with Charlie, "look at this contact,"

Bettie sadly looked at the app again and noticed how Charlie was constantly talking to another user called *Gender2*. Bettie didn't want to read them as she felt her breakfast and lunch start to crawl up her throat again.

"Find him," Bettie said.

"Find *her* you mean," Fran said. "The user might have used a VPN so I couldn't find their IP address, but photos on their profile gave me information about their phone. I eventually got a serial number and I know who owns it,"

"Who?" Bettie asked wanting back over to the SUV.

"Layla Taylor a local lecturer of religion at Kent University," Fran said.

Bettie slammed the door shut as the SUV roared away.

She was going to deal with Layla once and for all.

No one got away with attempted murder, not if she could help it.

***

20th November 2023

Hales Place, Canterbury, England

Bettie just grinned to herself as she walked down a very long main road just on the outskirts of Canterbury. The area used to be a massive council estate but mainly students used the small cheap houses as places to live.

Bettie rather liked the little white small houses that lined the wide road. A few blue, black and red cars drove past making a small cold breeze blow past her, only adding to the already bitter temperature surrounding her.

Bettie pulled her coat tight as she smiled at Layla Talyor who was currently getting out of her little black Fiat outside a small house. She had to admit Layla wasn't an awful-looking woman, she was skinny, attractive and her wavy black hair was probably attractive to a lot of men.

Including young male students.

"Layla Taylor," Bettie said.

"Um yes," she said looking at Bettie.

"Or should I call you *Gender2?*" Bettie asked. "It's hard to keep track of names, isn't it?"

Layla frowned. "I do not have time for this,"

Bettie took two large steps forward and closed the gap between her and Layla. Bettie wasn't allowing

Layla to get away.

"You incited a young man called Charlie to try and kill an innocent woman today," Bettie said.

"I don't know what you're talking about,"

Bettie just grinned. She liked difficult suspects because it meant she got to play with them, and hopefully that would give Fran more time to work with Sean and his boyfriend Harry on the computer stuff to find what she needed.

"Penelope was an innocent person. Why attack her and her group?" Bettie asked. "Because the bible told you to do it?"

Layla glared at Bettie. "How dare you. How dare you use the Bible in *that tone?*"

Bettie took a few steps away from her as she noticed the awful aroma of sweat and urine filling the space between them.

"I have my people investigating all your online activity as we speak. You might be able to explain away the extreme transphobia but what about your relationships with students?"

Bettie loved it how pale Layla went.

"You should technically be at work you know. It isn't 5 pm yet and why would you be going to a student's house?" Bettie asked.

Layla came over to her and Bettie felt a cold knife press against her stomach.

"Leave me alone,"

Bettie shook her head. She couldn't do that. There were innocent people and lives at stake. She wasn't going to back down.

"Then die bitch,"

A shot screamed through the air and Bettie just gasped as warm blood splattered over her face and her entire body went icy cold.

She slowly looked to her right and nodded her thanks as John stood a good twenty metres further up the road.

***

20th November 2023

London, England

Bettie still shook a little as she sat in the wonderfully warm, soft SUV as it slowly drove through the busy, packed and noisy streets of London later that night. The gentle humming of the SUV running, the loud honking of car horns and people shouting outside made Bettie smile a little.

This really was a typical night of traffic in London. John had asked about using the blue flashing lights but Bettie had shaken her head. She actually wanted the time to think.

She was already late for the medical conference but they were still allowing her to present whenever she got there. Bettie just didn't know if she could say anything worthy after today's events, the attempted murder and the death threat of Layla.

Bettie looked at Fran as she typed away on her laptop, probably finishing up their official statements for the Federation and the police. Then Bettie looked down at the small wooden box of amazing, delicious-looking Danish pastries that looked so good in between them. The rich aromas of strawberries filled the SUV.

Bettie reached down and picked one up, enjoying the touch of the buttery pastries as it coated her fingers in butter and rich icing. She was looking forward to having one of them after all.

"You feeling okay now?" Fran asked putting her laptop away.

Bettie shrugged. She had seen people die before in different situations but never exactly in front of her. She had seen her personal assistant die before in front of her but that situation had been different.

That was an assassination attempt not a killing done by her own security detail. Layla's death had to happen but Bettie never wanted it to happen though.

"I've sent the Federation's tech unit information about the app," Fran said. "They'll pass on everything to the police in time and we'll make sure the police deal with the hate website,"

"Thank you," Bettie said bringing the pastry closer to her lips. "I don't know what I'm going to say tonight,"

The car jerked a little as it hit a pothole.

Fran laughed. "Just do what you always do. Talk from the heart, and enjoy it. It's why the members love you talking and it's why I love listening to you,"

Bettie grinned and just nodded to herself because that was exactly right and that was exactly what she was going to do tonight. She might have been President of the Federation but that didn't mean she had to write official speeches.

She was a woman of the people and she was a woman of action. Bettie's place wasn't in some office, it was on the streets solving crimes, helping people and improving lives. She had never needed to write a speech.

"Use the blue lights now please,"

"Of course Madame President,"

Bettie just grinned as the SUV started its blue lights and they slowly started making progress through the traffic, because she had a speech to deliver to some medical and political folks.

Because it was Transgender Day of Remembrance. It might have been a day about honouring the murdered and dead trans people, amazing people whose lives had been cut too short. But there was a purpose as well.

It was making sure none of those people died in vain. So Bettie was going to go on that stage and she was going to convince people to help, support and improve transgender healthcare because everyone was entitled to healthcare, even trans people.

Because at the end of the day trans people were just people wanting to live a better life, which was what everyone wanted, so why should trans lives be harder or lesser than anyone else's?

They shouldn't.

And Bettie was so glad she had finally realised that simple point and that certainly helped to make today a day to remember. A day where she had solved a crime, saved lives and made sure a horrible transphobe could never hurt people ever again.

If that wasn't a day to remember then Bettie really wasn't sure what was.

BETTIE PRIVATE INVESTIGATOR SHORT STORY COLLECTION VOLUME 3

THE MYSTERY IN THE STUDENT HOUSE

10th January 2024

Canterbury, England

"My love for you is only matched by my contempt for you now auntie,"

Private Eye Bettie English playfully hit her favourite nephew in the entire world Sean, as they went into the awfully small white porch of the house they were secretly investigating. Bettie had to admit there was clearly a reason why these houses in this part of Canterbury were so cheap.

They were disgusting.

Bettie really didn't like the massive single panel of glass that covered three "walls" of the tiny porch, allowing out all the heat and allowing in the icy coldness of outside inside. It was so pointless. Even the red tile flooring was ugly, but Bettie supposed she couldn't complain.

It wasn't like she was actually here to help her

nephew check out a house. He had already graduated with his Masters, but the house owners didn't need to know that.

"Please take off your shoes," a woman said from inside the house.

Bettie rolled her eyes as the loud hammering of the rain pounded the thin tin roof above them, so much so Bettie could barely hear herself think. Let alone the woman.

All she wanted was a moment to warm up her hands, that were still aching and freezing from standing outside for ten minutes in the pouring rain waiting for the woman to show up. Bettie hated when people were late.

Bettie did as she was told and realised maybe it wasn't the best idea to wear boots today that went halfway up her shins. She knelt down on the icy cold floor and started untying her shoes.

Why this woman didn't have blue crime-scene shoe covers was beyond her. That would have made it so much easier for her to do this.

Bettie smiled at Sean as he just slipped off his shoes and leant against the doorframe just waiting for her. He ran a hand through his longish blond hair with tasteful pink highlights and he smiled at her.

She knew he was just as excited about the idea of trying to find DNA evidence as she was, because Sean was a brilliant private eye in his own right. It was just a shame he preferred the tech world to the private eye world.

Something she seriously wanted to change.

"This way," the woman said from inside the house.

Bettie put her shoes to one side and went into the tiny hallway. The overwhelming aroma of garlic, sweat and burnt toast hit her nose and Bettie coughed.

Even when she had been at university, her and her friends had never allowed the house to smell *this* bad. This was something else entirely, she just wanted to find something with DNA on and get the hell out of here.

She had been hired a few hours ago by a young university student, Rachel Pierce, from one of the more arty universities in Canterbury that reported she had been assaulted and *interfered* with coming home last night. She had gone through all the appropriate channels and reported her attacker to the police, but Rachel couldn't prove it.

So Bettie had tracked down Adam Green to this house, he was out enjoying his lectures whilst Rachel was with Bettie's boyfriend Graham trying to calm down and feel safe enough to return home.

Bettie flat out hated seeing Rachel like that, so she was going to do everything she could to put Adam away. He needed to pay and Bettie had to find DNA to match to what Rachel had given the police last night.

Bettie supposed the hallway itself wasn't that bad

with the tiny staircase to her left, a weird L-shaped bend that led to the living room judging by the floorplans (Bettie was still so grateful to her personal assistant Fran for them), and the dark blue fluffy carpet was rather pleasant.

Maybe the porch was the only bad part of the house.

The pounding of the rain behind her got even louder and Bettie pretended to smile as the realtor woman stepped into view and Bettie looked at her properly for the first time. She was rather young and pretty, which surprised Bettie because she sounded rough and a little tired on the phone. Instead the woman was tall, fit and stood in front of her like she was a bundle of energy.

Bettie knew the woman clearly didn't have kids, because Bettie had two twins and she was never going to look like that again. But she loved her twins more than anything in the entire world.

"What room are interested in seeing first? This is a wonderful home with so many amazing features, you and your friends are going to love it," the woman said to Sean. "My name's Caroline,"

Then Caroline looked at Bettie like it was a little weird she was here.

"I'm just here because his friends have lectures and they don't trust him to look at a house alone," Bettie said grinning.

Sean playfully poked his tongue out at her.

"Let's see the living room first," Sean said.

Bettie supposed that was a good place to start, she had to find something with DNA on. She really didn't want an attacker and potential assaulter to go free.

She had to get justice for the victim.

The awful aroma of burnt toast was even worse, if such a thing was possible, as Bettie followed Caroline into the large rectangular living room with dark white walls, two very ugly orange sofas and a smart TV hanging off (not on) the wall.

"We will obviously replace the TV before you move in," Caroline said clearly not knowing about the damage before today. "What are your thoughts?"

Bettie subtly nodded to Sean to signal she wanted to do some investigating and she wanted Caroline gone for a little while. So Sean started talking about the living room and how bad the damage was to the smart TV.

Then Sean subtly walked towards the floor-to-ceiling French doors at the end of the living room, so Caroline had to have her back to Bettie.

Bettie seriously did love her nephew, he was just brilliant.

The constant pounding of the rain hitting the French door covered Bettie's footsteps as she really focused on the living room. Including the two small wooden tables next to the sofas and there was a small black waste bin next to them in a corner.

Bettie went over to it. She knelt down and

managed to just about hide behind one of the ugly sofas and she just grinned at the waste bin because it was clearly fake.

The bin was simply filled with perfectly clean, not-used tissues that were barely roughed up enough to even remotely pass as used. Bettie just listened to Caroline cheerfully talk about the property and then she realised that there was an edge of panic in her voice.

Caroline was concerned about something and then Bettie didn't doubt the smart TV hanging off the walls wasn't concerning her. And she hadn't heard a single sound in the entire house, when her tenancy in her student house back in the late 00s was close to ending, Bettie had always made sure to be home when the new tenants came round. Mostly just because she was nosy and wanted to check out if any of them were hot, but also to make sure they didn't mess up anything.

Her friends had sadly experienced some problems back in the day, so she was determined to avoid a similar fate.

There was no one else in the house though and Bettie just couldn't understand why.

"Sean," Bettie said standing up and folding her arms, "no one lives here and Adam certainly isn't here,"

Caroline frowned. "What? What do you mean? Who the hell are you people?"

Sean laughed and gestured towards Bettie. "So not my department,"

Bettie took out her Private Eye ID card that also showed that she was the President of the British Private Eye Federation, a powerful organisation with more power than the governments of small countries.

Caroline took a few steps back. "I need to contact my boss. This isn't what I wanted. I don't want to deal with you people,"

Bettie took a few steps forward. "Caroline, I'm investigating a serious assault against a young woman last night and I need to find Adam, one of the tenants here,"

"Where is he?" Sean asked.

Bettie loved it how menacing and intimidating Sean was trying to look but it seriously wasn't working.

"I don't know," Caroline said taking out her phone. "He was meant to be here to let me in, that's why I was late. I had to drive back to the office to get the spare keys,"

Bettie went over to the Smart TV. It had clearly been pulled off the wall but it was at an angle with a slightly cracked screen, suggesting someone had been pushed into it and fell backwards.

"What about the other tenants?" Bettie asked. "My assistant said there were four people living here,"

Caroline shook slightly and Bettie went over and placed a gentle hand on her shoulder.

"I don't know," Caroline said. "This... this is all

a bit much. Can I just call me boss?"

Bettie just looked at Sean. He subtly smiled at her and Bettie liked that smile, because they both knew this case was just about to get started and that excited her a lot more than she wanted to admit even to herself.

"Don't bother," Bettie said, "I'll get my assistant to find your tenants and hopefully your employer can get their rent,"

"Thank you," Caroline said.

Bettie shook her head as she put her boots back on because she couldn't believe that Caroline sounded like she was only interested in rent and not the lives of the tenants that could be in danger because if Bettie had learnt anything over her career. It was never to underestimate how dark situations could get.

Little did Bettie realise just how true that idea was.

***

Bettie nodded her thanks to Fran as she passed Bettie a large mug of piping hot ground coffee as soon as she came into the living room of her house. Bettie loved how the rich, intense aromas of real coffee filled the large living room, instead of the instant rubbish she had been buying lately to save money. Not because she needed to save but it meant she could donate to charities even more.

"Mummy," Elizabeth said as she charged at Bettie.

Bettie flat out loved her little 16-month-old bundle of joy. Elizabeth was the most beautiful, precious and most amazing kid she had ever met and Bettie really did love both her kids equally. She was also rather impressed Graham had dressed Elizabeth properly today instead of letting her run around in PJs like he normally did.

Not that she could blame him because both the twins were so cute in their PJs.

Bettie picked up her beautiful daughter and hugged her tight after putting the coffee mug on the large walnut coffee table in the middle of the living room. At least she didn't have to go out in that awful rain that was still hammering outside.

Then Bettie nodded at the three massive white boards Fran had thankfully put up whilst Bettie had driven over here. The white boards were pushed against the far wall of the room so she couldn't see the TV but that didn't matter. She was here to solve a crime, not watch TV.

The whiteboard to the left was covered in notes about Rachel and the attack last night using everything they had gotten from the police report, Rachel herself and any other evidence they could find.

Bettie had to admit she would have liked a lot more detail on that particular board, but this was a tough one. They only knew Rachel was attacked in an alley by Adam and then she had managed to run to the police station before breaking down, crying and succumbing to shock.

Thankfully she had managed to give her statement first. Bettie was really impressed with how brave, amazing and courageous Rachel had been. She doubted she could hold off shock and crying that much.

"I can't actually find that much on the other tenants," Fran said sitting down on one of Bettie's two massive sofas.

Bettie smiled as Sean and his wonderful boyfriend Harry came down the stairs holding hands before sitting on another sofa.

Having her wonderful family here made Bettie a lot more excited than she had any right to feel because now she knew, truly knew they were going to find Adam and the other tenants. Together her and her family and friends were unstoppable.

"I could only find references and odd social media posts about the other tenants. Joshua, Nathan and Ethan all lived in that house yesterday," Fran said. "But today, no one has seen them,"

"Doorbell footage?" Bettie asked bouncing Elizabeth a little in her arms.

"Nothing," Harry said.

Bettie rolled her eyes. If there was doorbell footage of the tenants then Harry would have found it, so Bettie had no reason to doubt it. It was just annoying as hell these tenants looked like they had simply disappeared.

"Auntie, why would the tenants leave?"

Bettie smiled. "What connections are there between Rachel and Adam and the other tenants? I know they all go to the same university and Rachel and Adam had seen each other at clubs and bars before,"

"That's it," Fran said shrugging. "My initial and secondary searches all reveal there are no other connections. No classes, no social groups and nothing else that links Rachel to Adam or anyone else,"

"How did she know his name?" Harry asked.

Bettie smiled as everyone went deadly silent and she just let the question hang in the air between them all. That was a brilliant question and she wished she had thought of it herself because it was stupidly true.

Fran was an amazing computer person and personal assistant, and Bettie believed her when Fran said the searches came up blank. Bettie had little doubt Harry had done a computer deep dive on Adam, Rachel and the tenants because he was sensational with computers.

All the searches had come up blank, so why did Rachel know Adam's name? And why was she able to identify him as her attacker?

Bettie gestured Sean to come with her and then Bettie gave Elizabeth a little kiss on the cheek before giving her to Harry.

Then Bettie and Sean went upstairs into Sean's and Harry's bedroom where the subtle aromas of lavender, lilacs and roses filled the large bedroom from a little romantic gesture from Harry to Sean yesterday.

Bettie smiled at how clean, tidy and filled with great personal items like holiday photos and romantic gifts covered all the walls and cabinets. It was why she had wanted Rachel to be in here today, because it was such a happy room filled with love, protection and devotion between lovers.

It was a safe place.

"Hi," Graham said in his tight sexy jeans and tight black hoody (Bettie was so taking that off later on), where Rachel was playing with Harrison.

Bettie had to admit it was great seeing Rachel smiling, laughing and with a little more colour back in her face. Bettie had hated seeing Rachel this morning with cuts, bruises and extreme fear on her face.

She didn't even want to question Rachel now but she was going to have to, the case might depend on it.

"Harrison," Bettie said as joyfully as she could, "can you show Sean where the ice lollies are please? He's forgotten again,"

Cute little Harrison sat up immediately and started wiggling towards the end of Sean's bed before jumping off with so much energy Bettie was almost scared.

"Sean's so silly isn't he mummy?" Harrison asked.

"Yes he is sweetie,"

Bettie laughed as Harrison just gently took Sean's hand in his and he led Sean back down up.

"Mummy!" Harrison shouted, "can I have one if I do this!"

"Yes sweetie and make sure your sister gets one,"

"Okay. Thank you mummy,"

Bettie laughed and Graham just shook his head at her. Then Bettie frowned a little as she went over to Rachel and sat on the opposite end of the bed to her.

"Rachel I need to ask you a simple question, is that okay?" Bettie asked.

Rachel looked at the floor. "I've already told Graham everything I know,"

"I know but it's important," Bettie said knowing Graham had been trained to talk to assault victims so if she had said anything major then he would have told her by now.

"Please," Graham said. "Bettie is an amazing woman and she will help you, but remember like I said, you need to trust us,"

Rachel nodded so Bettie weakly smiled at Rachel. "How do you know Adam? We can't find any record or evidence of you knowing each other? He never spoke to you at the bar, you don't share classes, social groups or anything,"

Rachel looked up at Bettie. "You calling me a liar,"

"No," Bettie said shaking her head. "I'm just curious and a defence barrister will be a lot harsher than me when this goes to trial,"

Rachel laid down on the bed and buried her face

in the pillows.

Bettie wanted to move closer and gently hold Rachel's hand but she didn't dare, and she couldn't help but feel that something was off.

"I met him once," Rachel said. "It was first year, so two years ago, there was a rave near the River Medway. No phones, no tech and no cameras,"

Bettie nodded. She had heard about the rave because the police had broken it up and it was on a small sea fort island in the river Medway near Upnor and Hoo Marina.

It had been a massive rave and no one could exactly figure out how over 100 young people had gotten on the island in the first place, but after the drugs were found, high-price lawyers for the rich kids had brought down their power on the police and whatnot, no one had ever thought about it again.

"I was swinging from one of the rope swings and Adam started chatting to me. He was nice, sweet and we exchanged names and whatnot," Rachel said. "Then he tried to kiss me and I said no. He wasn't happy,"

Bettie nodded at Graham.

"Then I saw him last night for the first time since the rave. He was happy to see me and I tried to get away from him but… it didn't work out, did it?"

Bettie got off the bed and paced around a little. At least that was the connection and why Rachel was able to identify the attacker, but there were still more questions. Thankfully, she only needed to ask Rachel one more.

"Joshua, Nathan and Ethan, they live with Adam," Bettie said. "I need to know would any of them fight Adam to protect you,"

Rachel sat up on the bed and smiled. "Ethan would, bless him, he was so cute. Adam hated him for being a transman but no one else cares. He was so cute, so sweet and so… perfect,"

Bettie smiled. It was great to know how much she cared about Ethan, and that explained a lot about what had happened last night.

"Final question," Bettie said, "I'm guessing you and Ethan met at the rave and you haven't spoken since,"

"I wanted to get his phone number that night but Adam was so focused on me, I just couldn't. I didn't even realise he was trying to control me that night," Rachel said then she threw her head back and accidently hit the headboard.

Bettie nodded because things were finally starting to make perfect sense. She didn't doubt for a moment that after the attack Adam had gone home to his housemates, bragged about the attack then Ethan would have been outraged.

Then Bettie completely understood if Ethan was angry enough to start a fight and him or Adam or maybe one of the others had been pushed into the smart TV, causing the damage.

It was only what happened next Bettie didn't

understand yet.

Why stage the property to look like it was being lived in when it clearly wasn't? Why not just run instead of preparing the scene like the waste bin? It made no sense.

Bettie took out her phone and called the Federation, she was going to need a helicopter.

She had to get to the sea fort immediately. She didn't know how but she just knew Adam and the others would be there.

And Bettie was going to get the truth out of Adam no matter what.

***

Bettie flat out loved the power, resources and all the good vehicles the Federation had access to as she waved the massive black helicopter away after it had carefully dropped her off next to Fort Darrett in the River Medway via rope winch.

The soft wild grass was soft and rather warm for a change under Bettie's feet and she was so glad the damn rain had stopped about two hours ago, so her boots weren't getting wet. The very last thing she wanted was to be stuck on an island when it was wet and cold and just draining.

The Fort itself was rather impressive with it being a massive ring of concrete and bricks going up one storey with a flat roof. Yet because the Fort had been designed for 11 guns, there were 11 flat sides to the ring with wide openings to shoot through.

Even though the Fort never saw any action.

Bettie was glad it was in such good condition considering it had finished being built in 1872 as part of plans for the defences of Chatham Dockyard where England had kept most of its naval power in the 1800s.

Bettie just couldn't help but smile at the old Fort because she wanted to know what the Fort could have been if the original ideas for two tiers had been completed. The cost of the project had caused it to be finished in 1872 and it was impressive enough, but Bettie would have liked to know what it could have been.

The rich aromas of sea salt, smoke and cooked meat filled the air as Bettie went over to the small hole in a massive rusty sheet of metal that had been placed over each gun opening.

Bettie could hear muttered voices and she really hoped that Graham, Sean and Fran could convince Kent Police to bring officers here as soon as possible.

She was about to climb inside when she noticed the wide moat around the Fort that dropped down into thick, sloppy mud below with steep sides on either side. The only way to get to the Fort was by climbing over a thick wooden beam and even that was only accessible after coming through a narrow opening through a thick bush of thorns that ran around the edge of the entire moat.

If Bettie got into trouble here then she was completely alone.

Bettie climbed inside and was surprised at the sheer grey stone curved walls of the Fort that went round in a ring. There was so much *stuff* on the ground like dust, sand and dirt that it was like nature was determined more than ever to reclaim the island.

Then she saw them.

In the middle of the Fort there was another moat that Bettie knew from her childhood dropped down tens upon tens of metres to flooded storage rooms. But after the drop-down, there was a large brick platform covered in bushes and trees and the people she was searching for were there.

Bettie recognised Adam immediately with his black crewcut, black eye and almost too-thin body. Then there were two other young men she couldn't really tell apart with brown hair and matching black clothes, they had to be Joshua and Nathan.

But it was Ethan that Bettie was more concerned about.

The young man with longish blond hair was holding his left arm like he had been stabbed and his once-blue hoody was now a lot darker, and Bettie just hated Adam more than ever.

Bettie went over to the edge of the moat and she was right next to a narrow brick walkway that led onto the central platform where the others were.

"Who the hell are you?" Adam asked clearly annoyed.

"She's Bettie English," Ethan said a little

starstruck. "You know, the woman in the papers and the woman on the news. You're in shit now Adam,"

Bettie laughed because hopefully Ethan was right.

"You attacked Rachel last night, you committed criminal damage in your house and I'm sure this is private property. How did you even get here?"

Everyone looked at Bettie like she was the dumbest woman alive.

"There's a guy in Hoo Marina," Adam said, "you pay him and he brings you after dark,"

Bettie nodded and kicked some of the dust under her feet. At least that explained how all the students got here for the rave two years ago and how the four of them had gotten here after the attack.

"What happened at the house?" Bettie asked wanting to buy the police as much time as possible.

Adam pulled out a knife that was still dripping blood.

"It don't matter," Adam said. "None of this matters. Just leave us alone and go away,"

"I can't do that Adam and you know it. You attacked an innocent woman,"

Bettie went onto the brick walkway and hated how a massive brick splashed into the water below. She wasn't sure how long this walkway would hold but she wasn't going to show Adam she was scared.

Adam grabbed Ethan's injured arm and pressed the knife against his throat.

"This is all your fault you bitch. Why don't you

just admit you like Rachel? But we both know she won't like a pussy girl like you. You aren't even a real man,"

Bettie just glared at Adam. That was enough and she was going to make Adam pay for everything now.

Bettie took another step forward and two massive bricks splashed into the water below.

She went to get onto the platform but Joshua and Nathan picked up two broken bricks each and gestured they were going to throw them at Bettie.

Bettie seriously wasn't sure if she could dodge all four bricks without falling into the stagnant water below. She hated to imagine what disease or infection she would pick up from that water.

Adam jabbed the knife a little harder against Ethan's throat and Bettie hated seeing how defeated Ethan looked.

"She likes you a lot Ethan," Bettie said. "She doesn't care that you're a transman and you are a man to her, and me for what it's worth. People like Adam don't matter,"

Ethan looked into Bettie's eyes. "Really?"

"Her face lit up when she spoke about you," Bettie said.

Police sirens echoed around the Fort from the distance.

Ethan stomped on Adam's feet.
Adam let go. He was about to swing.
Bettie charged forward.

The walkway collapsed.

Bettie screamed.

She fell.

She gripped onto the edge of the central platform as the bricks splashed down below.

Bettie kicked against the wall but she couldn't get a grip.

Thunder roared overhead and rain started slashing down. The edge of the platform was getting wetter and wetter.

Bettie didn't know how much longer she could hold onto it.

"Leave her," Adam shouted.

Bettie tried to pull herself up as much as she could but she couldn't.

Her hands burnt. Her muscles ached. Pain flooded her arms.

She was about to let go.

Bettie shouted for help. No one came. She was alone. She was going to fall.

She fell.

Two hands gripped her arm.

Bettie slammed into the brick wall as someone pulled her up.

As soon as she felt the solid central platform under her she leapt up and hugged Ethan.

Then she broke the hug and listened for the police sirens. They were coming from the south side of the island and no other direction.

"The man gave us a crappy little speedboat on

the north side of the island," Ethan said. "Is that important?"

Bettie nodded and she ran and jumped over the moat she had just almost died from. She rushed over to the nearest gun opening and climbed outside.

Ethan followed her.

Bettie started running towards the thick wooden beam. "Of course it's important. Even a crappy speedboat with a two-stroke engine would let them get to the mainland,"

Bettie went running and she went quickly and carefully as she got over the wooden beam that moaned and groaned as she went over it.

Bettie hissed in pain as the sharp thorns caught her as she raced through the narrow opening. The awfully soft ground was almost trying to slow her down but Bettie wasn't stopping for anything or anyone.

As soon as she got through the thorn bushes she saw Adam, Nathan and Joshua on the other side of a large area of cord grass. They were climbing into a small black speedboat that barely looked seaworthy.

They were going to die if they went out in that. Bettie couldn't allow that to happen.

Bettie ran as fast as she could.

The thick aroma of sea salt was almost choking but she kept running.

Icy cold breeze slammed against her but Bettie just kept running. Ethan ran behind her but Bettie was faster.

Bettie could barely hear the police sirens of the police boats as Adam pushed the boat into the water. Just as Joshua and Nathan were about to climb in Adam pushed them out.

Joshua and Nathan slipped on the mud and accidentally pushed the boat out into the raging River Medway.

The rain lashed down even harder and Adam activated the engine. The speedboat roared to life.

Bettie ran as fast as she could. But Adam just started to speed away.

A massive gust of icy wind made Bettie jump and created massive waves in the river. One slammed into the speedboat.

Flipping it over.

Bettie didn't think. She only acted. She charged into the River Medway and swam towards Adam.

She wasn't letting him drown.

He had to answer for his crimes.

***

A few hours later when the awful rain had finally stopped, Bettie wrapped a wonderfully thick white blanket round herself as she sat on her sofa facing the TV in her living room. When she had gotten home from the hospital where she had been treated for hyperthermia, given god knows how many statements to the police and been slightly told off by Graham for swimming into icy cold water during a storm, she had felt like the house was a little empty.

The three massive whiteboards were gone, Fran had gone home for the night and even Sean and Harry had gone out with some friends tonight. They had tried to paint it as a crazy night on the town, but Bettie knew it was code for just talking, laughing and enjoying themselves at a local pub.

Bettie had put the twins to bed earlier and she was just enjoying the silence of the house after a wonderfully hectic day. So Bettie allowed the softness of the sofa to claim her weight and she was so looking forward to what was going to happen next.

Especially with the delicious rich aromas of basil, garlic and cheese coming from the kitchen where Graham was finishing up one of his "famous" meals for her. Sometimes that meant great food from recipes from mainland Europe or sometimes it meant disgusting creations of his own, but Bettie loved him no matter what.

She was just hoping beyond hope it would be the first option.

After she had swam into the River Medway, getting colder and colder with each passing second, she had managed to grab Adam despite his shock and dragged him back to the island Fort Darnett was on. Then she had handed them all over to Graham and the police and they had gone to hospital to be checked out.

Bettie was glad she had only needed to be warmed up with more tea (not coffee sadly) than she wanted to admit. She so wasn't drinking English tea after that hospital trip, it was disgusting.

At least Adam had confessed (and DNA confirmed) to seeing Rachel at the party last night then he had followed her on her way home and when she had taken a shortcut down an alley, he had attacked her. Bettie had almost vomited during his graphic account of the attack.

She never wanted him to see the light of day ever again.

Then Adam had gone home after kicking Rachel in the stomach to see his housemates. He had bragged about it because it made him feel powerful and manly so Ethan had flipped out at him for attacking an innocent woman. Especially a woman that had been so kind to him.

They had fought and Ethan had been pushed into the smart TV making it hang off the wall. So Joshua and Nathan being Adam's good little pets had sided with Adam and made Ethan help with the staging of the house.

The idea behind that had been to give them a day to decide what to do with Ethan and where they were going to run away to. They knew Rachel was going to talk so their time was limited.

Bettie was still surprised they had gone to the Fort but considering that was where all of this had started two years ago, it sort of made sense and Bettie probably would have done the same if she was them.

Once at the Fort Adam had started a small fire to

keep them warm and Ethan had tried to get Adam to turn himself in. Adam had slashed Ethan's arm to make him shut up.

Then Bettie arrived and judging by the sheer look of anger on Adam's face at the hospital when Ethan had walked past his bed, she didn't doubt Ethan would have been dead if she hadn't arrived.

Bettie was more than glad she had. Especially because Rachel had gone to the hospital to see Ethan and they had spoken, kissed and they had agreed to go on a date.

Bettie couldn't stop smiling as the man she loved came into the living room without any food and a massive guilty grin on his face. He might have been a rubbish chef but she loved him more than anything else in the entire world.

"Let me guess," Bettie said, "takeaway and sex tonight?"

"You read my mind,"

Bettie threw the blanket at Graham as they laughed and kissed and made out like two horny teenagers. And after the hecticness of today, Bettie was more than looking forward to all the fun she was going to have tonight and all the nights after that.

GET YOUR FREE SHORT STORY NOW! And get signed up to Connor Whiteley's newsletter to hear about new gripping books, offers and exciting projects. (You'll never be sent spam)

https://www.subscribepage.io/wintersignup

About the author:

Connor Whiteley is the author of over 60 books in the sci-fi fantasy, nonfiction psychology and books for writer's genre and he is a Human Branding Speaker and Consultant.

He is a passionate warhammer 40,000 reader, psychology student and author.

Who narrates his own audiobooks and he hosts The Psychology World Podcast.

All whilst studying Psychology at the University of Kent, England.

Also, he was a former Explorer Scout where he gave a speech to the Maltese President in August 2018 and he attended Prince Charles' 70th Birthday Party at Buckingham Palace in May 2018.

Plus, he is a self-confessed coffee lover!

OTHER SHORT STORIES BY CONNOR WHITELEY

<u>Mystery Short Stories:</u>

Protecting The Woman She Hated

Finding A Royal Friend

Our Woman In Paris

Corrupt Driving

A Prime Assassination

Jubilee Thief

Jubilee, Terror, Celebrations

Negative Jubilation

Ghostly Jubilation

Killing For Womenkind

A Snowy Death

Miracle Of Death

A Spy In Rome

The 12:30 To St Pancreas

A Country In Trouble

A Smokey Way To Go

A Spicy Way To GO

A Marketing Way To Go

A Missing Way To Go

A Showering Way To Go

Poison In The Candy Cane

Christmas Innocence

You Better Watch Out

Christmas Theft

Trouble In Christmas

Smell of The Lake

Problem In A Car

BETTIE PRIVATE INVESTIGATOR SHORT STORY COLLECTION VOLUME 3

Theft, Past and Team
Embezzler In The Room
A Strange Way To Go
A Horrible Way To Go
Ann Awful Way To Go
An Old Way To Go
A Fishy Way To Go
A Pointy Way To Go
A High Way To Go
A Fiery Way To Go
A Glassy Way To Go
A Chocolatey Way To Go
Kendra Detective Mystery Collection Volume 1
Kendra Detective Mystery Collection Volume 2
Stealing A Chance At Freedom
Glassblowing and Death
Theft of Independence
Cookie Thief
Marble Thief
Book Thief
Art Thief
Mated At The Morgue
The Big Five Whoopee Moments
Stealing An Election
Mystery Short Story Collection Volume 1
Mystery Short Story Collection Volume 2
Criminal Performance
Candy Detectives
Key To Birth In The Past

Science Fiction Short Stories:
Temptation
Superhuman Autopsy
Blood In The Redwater
All Is Dust
Vigil
Emperor Forgive Us
Their Brave New World
Gummy Bear Detective
The Candy Detective
What Candies Fear
The Blurred Image
Shattered Legions
The First Rememberer
Life of A Rememberer
System of Wonder
Lifesaver
Remarkable Way She Died
The Interrogation of Annabella Stormic
Blade of The Emperor
Arbiter's Truth
Computation of Battle
Old One's Wrath
Puppets and Masters
Ship of Plague
Interrogation
Edge of Failure
One Way Choice
Acceptable Losses
Balance of Power

BETTIE PRIVATE INVESTIGATOR SHORT STORY COLLECTION VOLUME 3

Good Idea At The Time
Escape Plan
Escape In The Hesitation
Inspiration In Need
Singing Warriors
Knowledge is Power
Killer of Polluters
Climate of Death
The Family Mailing Affair
Defining Criminality
The Martian Affair
A Cheating Affair
The Little Café Affair
Mountain of Death
Prisoner's Fight
Claws of Death
Bitter Air
Honey Hunt
Blade On A Train
<u>Fantasy Short Stories:</u>
City of Snow
City of Light
City of Vengeance
Dragons, Goats and Kingdom
Smog The Pathetic Dragon
Don't Go In The Shed
The Tomato Saver
The Remarkable Way She Died
The Bloodied Rose

Asmodia's Wrath
Heart of A Killer
Emissary of Blood
Dragon Coins
Dragon Tea
Dragon Rider
Sacrifice of the Soul
Heart of The Flesheater
Heart of The Regent
Heart of The Standing
Feline of The Lost
Heart of The Story
City of Fire
Awaiting Death

<u>Other books by Connor Whiteley:</u>
<u>Bettie English Private Eye Series</u>
A Very Private Woman
The Russian Case
A Very Urgent Matter
A Case Most Personal
Trains, Scots and Private Eyes
The Federation Protects

<u>Lord of War Origin Trilogy:</u>
Not Scared Of The Dark
Madness
Burn It All

BETTIE PRIVATE INVESTIGATOR SHORT STORY COLLECTION VOLUME 3

<u>The Fireheart Fantasy Series</u>
Heart of Fire
Heart of Lies
Heart of Prophecy
Heart of Bones
Heart of Fate

<u>City of Assassins (Urban Fantasy)</u>
City of Death
City of Martyrs
City of Pleasure
City of Power

<u>Agents of The Emperor</u>
Return of The Ancient Ones
Vigilance
Angels of Fire
Kingmaker
The Eight
The Lost Generation
<u>Lord Of War Trilogy (Agents of The Emperor)</u>
Not Scared Of The Dark
Madness
Burn It All Down

<u>The Garro Series- Fantasy/Sci-fi</u>
GARRO: GALAXY'S END
GARRO: RISE OF THE ORDER
GARRO: END TIMES

GARRO: SHORT STORIES
GARRO: COLLECTION
GARRO: HERESY
GARRO: FAITHLESS
GARRO: DESTROYER OF WORLDS
GARRO: COLLECTIONS BOOK 4-6
GARRO: MISTRESS OF BLOOD
GARRO: BEACON OF HOPE
GARRO: END OF DAYS

Winter Series- Fantasy Trilogy Books
WINTER'S COMING
WINTER'S HUNT
WINTER'S REVENGE
WINTER'S DISSENSION

Miscellaneous:
RETURN
FREEDOM
SALVATION
Reflection of Mount Flame
The Masked One
The Great Deer

Gay Romance Novellas
Breaking, Nursing, Repiaring A Broken Heart
Jacob And Daniel
Fallen For A Lie
His Heartstopper
Spying And Weddings

BETTIE PRIVATE INVESTIGATOR SHORT STORY COLLECTION VOLUME 3

<u>All books in 'An Introductory Series':</u>

Careers In Psychology

Psychology of Suicide

Dementia Psychology

Clinical Psychology Reflections Volume 4

Forensic Psychology of Terrorism And Hostage-Taking

Forensic Psychology of False Allegations

Year In Psychology

CBT For Anxiety

CBT For Depression

Applied Psychology

BIOLOGICAL PSYCHOLOGY 3RD EDITION

COGNITIVE PSYCHOLOGY THIRD EDITION

SOCIAL PSYCHOLOGY- 3RD EDITION

ABNORMAL PSYCHOLOGY 3RD EDITION

PSYCHOLOGY OF RELATIONSHIPS- 3RD EDITION

DEVELOPMENTAL PSYCHOLOGY 3RD EDITION

HEALTH PSYCHOLOGY

RESEARCH IN PSYCHOLOGY

A GUIDE TO MENTAL HEALTH AND TREATMENT AROUND THE WORLD- A GLOBAL LOOK AT DEPRESSION

FORENSIC PSYCHOLOGY

THE FORENSIC PSYCHOLOGY OF THEFT, BURGLARY AND OTHER CRIMES AGAINST PROPERTY

CRIMINAL PROFILING: A FORENSIC PSYCHOLOGY GUIDE TO FBI PROFILING AND GEOGRAPHICAL AND STATISTICAL PROFILING.
CLINICAL PSYCHOLOGY
FORMULATION IN PSYCHOTHERAPY
PERSONALITY PSYCHOLOGY AND INDIVIDUAL DIFFERENCES
CLINICAL PSYCHOLOGY REFLECTIONS VOLUME 1
CLINICAL PSYCHOLOGY REFLECTIONS VOLUME 2
Clinical Psychology Reflections Volume 3
CULT PSYCHOLOGY
Police Psychology

A Psychology Student's Guide To University
How Does University Work?
A Student's Guide To University And Learning
University Mental Health and Mindset

www.ingramcontent.com/pod-product-compliance
Lightning Source LLC
LaVergne TN
LVHW011844060526
838200LV00054B/4151